UNEXPECTED

WENDY SMITH

Edited by
LAUREN CLARKE

Cover Design by
MOSS BOOK COVERS

 Formatted with Vellum

DEDICATION

This book is dedicated to my father Arthur Frederikson.
21 June 1941 - 18 March 2016.

They shall grow not old, as we that are left
grow old:
Age shall not weary them, nor the years
condemn.
At the going down of the sun and in the
morning,
We will remember them.

ONE

I HATED MORNINGS. I dragged my butt out of bed, and staggered to the bathroom to wake up and start my day. My shoulder-length brown hair was fashioned into a bob. It was supposed to be easy to maintain, but every morning became a new challenge to untangle the knots that magically appeared overnight.

Grimacing as the brush hit each snag, I studied myself in the mirror. My recent thirtieth birthday had been hard to deal with. Could you have a mid-life crisis at thirty? As I brushed, I leaned forward to examine my skin, checking for any sign of wrinkles. If I found a new one, it was enough to make me fly into a panic, then work out a new way to apply my makeup to cover it.

After applying my makeup, I took the short walk to the end of the street to catch the bus. Despite being five-foot-eight, I wore six-inch stilettos. Why on earth I kept tormenting myself with those things I had no idea, but at least

I'd be off my feet on the way into the city toward work and only had to walk a short distance at the other end.

Every day I approached the building and sighed. When I'd started working for Jameson Interiors three years ago, I'd been keen to make a difference and create the most beautifully decorated rooms that had ever existed.

The reality was quite different.

It wasn't taxing—in fact, at times it seemed like I was paid for colouring in, but it was a job, and I needed every dollar I could get.

The morning dragged. By ten a.m. it felt as if I'd been at work all day.

"Nicola. Want to go for coffee?" Tamara was the last person who should suggest that. It might sound like bragging, but I could run rings around her designing interiors.

"Only if you promise that it's going to make the day go faster." I chewed on the end of my pencil, looking at the clock for the billionth time.

Tamara stood, leaning over my desk. "If we go to that little place downstairs, I'll buy you one of those chocolate slices that you like. That's got to help."

I sighed, placing my pencil on the desk. "You talked me into it."

She grinned, nodding slowly. "I know how to get you out of that chair. Works every time. Shame it's the only time you eat anything slightly unhealthy."

I stood, placing my hands on my waist. "Got to stay trim somehow."

As she turned, I caught her rolling her eyes. How could I blame her? I'd spent years in the quest for perfection, losing weight to the point where my friends worried about it, then gaining just a little to stop them judging.

"Let's go before Madam Bitchface comes out and gives us some more work to do."

I grinned. "Race you."

We ran toward the door, waving goodbye to Cherie, the receptionist, and bumping into one another as we hit the frame and emerging on the other side, giggling as we made our way to the lifts.

"Doing anything at the weekend?" Tamara asked.

"Don't know. Probably not. Might go see Mum and Dad." I yawned as I pressed the button. "Though staying at home and sleeping is kinda tempting."

"Tell me about it. I'll probably be trying to catch up on work."

The doors opened, and we slipped in, leaning against the rail that lined the walls. Tamara pressed the ground floor button, and slowly the ancient elevator creaked and groaned its way down.

"One day, we'll get in this thing and fall straight to the floor." She laughed, but there had to be some truth in that. It was way overdue for an upgrade.

"Yeah, well there's no chance of Renee upgrading us to a decent building. This one'll collapse around our ears before that happens."

We both took jabs at our boss, but truth was that we both needed our jobs. I don't know how Renee Jameson had stayed in business so long. In my opinion, she was a talent-free zone. She hadn't created anything for herself in years, and never touched a design until it was so far down the track that any minor changes wouldn't hurt it.

"One day, you'll have your own design company and I'll come and work for you." Tamara smiled. Her words touched my heart, even though I knew that wasn't likely any time soon. I was too dependent on this job to pay my rent to walk away and start something new.

We hit the ground floor. Literally. I gripped the rail tight, even though we'd come to a stop. I'd been in these elevators a million times, but I still failed to anticipate the landing. The doors opened out into the lobby, and Tamara and I stumbled out on shaky legs.

"Those lifts suck *so* much," she said.

"You know we have this conversation every time we come down here."

She laughed. "We'll continue to have this conversation every day we come down here."

The coffee shop was in the lobby. We checked out the food in the cabinet, Tamara pointing at various things. "Can I please have a latte?" I asked.

"Me too, and two of those chocolate slices." Tamara leaned over my shoulder.

I didn't know what I would do without Tamara. She helped keep my sanity.

We hid away in a corner, clutching our coffees in take-away cups. If Renee turned up, she'd give us her evil witch glare.

"I saw a junior job advertised over at Practical Interiors. I thought about applying for it." Tamara sipped her coffee.

"You so should. If it's paying a decent amount of money."

A junior role would be paying less than I was currently paid, otherwise I'd have looked at it myself.

She screwed up her face. "I don't know if I can be bothered going through the whole interviewing process. Plus, I don't want to leave you alone."

"You are very sweet, but you have to look after yourself. If it's a good opportunity, go for it." I took a bite of the chocolate slice, closing my eyes at the sweet taste. I didn't indulge often —it was hard enough sometimes to scrape together enough to keep up my coffee habit.

"Hmm maybe ..." She sighed. "We should get back."

I checked my watch. "Yeah. If we stay too long we'll never hear the end of it."

"I'm just going to pop across the road and get some hot chips." Tamara stood. "I'll meet you back at the elevator? I'll be about two minutes."

"Sure."

As she walked off and disappeared into the building across the street, for a moment, I thought about following. *Can't be bothered.* Instead I turned, setting off across the lobby.

Halfway across, I paused. Coming out of the lift was a man with a familiar face. My friend Rebecca's dad.

He stopped not far from me to shake the hand of the man who had accompanied him. As he turned toward the exit, his gaze landed on me.

"Nicola?" He smiled, his eyes flashing with recognition. I should think so. There was a time in my teenage years when I'd spent a lot of weekends in his home. We didn't see him a lot; he worked hard and was often absent with his child's life, having a nanny around at lot of the time. But I'd know him anywhere. He didn't look much different than he had back then.

"Hey, Mr Wallace."

"It's been a while. How are you keeping? How are your parents? Are they still on that farm?"

I nodded. "We're all well. I see Mum and Dad from time to time. How are you?"

He smiled widely. "Just great. Do you work around here?"

I pointed up. "Level twelve. Jameson Interiors."

"Ahhh. An artist like your parents?"

Shaking my head, I grinned. "I didn't inherit all their skills. I'm an interior designer."

His eyebrows crept up, and that gaze of his, so much like Rebecca's when she was after information, was pretty intense. "Do you do office refits, things like that?"

"Mostly. Sometimes homes but mostly businesses."

"Sounds interesting." *Yeah whatever.* Barely anyone wanted to hear me blab on about colours and textures. Not even the people I worked with at times.

"I think so."

He smiled, and my stomach flip-flopped.

When did he become so nice? It was so hard to imagine that he was around the same age as my father, too. What was that—fifty-something? He obviously took care of himself.

Rebecca went to the gym every lunchtime except for the one day a month we all met at Le Grande. Maybe he followed her lead.

"Well, it was very nice seeing you again, Nicola. Take care of yourself."

"You too."

One last smile and he was gone. I watched as he walked toward the exit, sighing a little at the way he carried himself. Good-looking, professional, way out of my league and ...

What am I thinking? That's Rebecca's father.

I barely noticed Tamara drawing level.

"Who's he?" she asked, chewing a chip in my ear as she came in close.

"A friend."

"He can be my friend if he wants." She giggled, and I rolled my eyes.

"Actually he's the father of one of my best friends."

Her eyes widened. "Seriously? He didn't look that old."

I shrugged. "To be honest, I think he looks the same as he did when I was a kid. I don't think he's aged a bit."

Tamara grabbed my hand, pulling me toward the elevator. "Let's stop staring and get back to work before we hear all about it."

As I stepped in and turned, I caught one last glimpse of Rebecca's father. He'd stopped at the exit and had looked back toward me.

My heart pounded as his gaze met mine, the metal doors sliding together to cut in between us like an unwanted intruder.

I stood still for a moment, willing the doors to open again, but what was the point?

It wasn't like he'd be feeling the same way.

BY MID-AFTERNOON, I was in deep in concentration, working on a colour scheme. I loved this part of my job—working out what colours went where, what materials would look best. The only thing better was getting my hands on a project. In design school, the best part was the creating, not the planning. In this job, I didn't get to do that.

"Nicola." Tamara made a weird squeaky, hissy noise. I'd been lost in my work. I looked up at her, confused.

"What's your problem?"

She waggled her eyebrows. I froze, then slowly turned to look behind me. Renee stood there, watching over my shoulder.

"Renee?"

"I've just had a potential client on the phone. He says he knows you."

"Oh?"

"Neil Wallace. Wallace Finance."

I nodded, flicking back to the memory of earlier in the day. *Rebecca's dad.*

"He's asked for you. Apparently he knows how talented your father is and thinks it's rubbed off on you." Her tone was civil enough. Inside, she'd be seething at him asking for one of her workers by name and not her, even though we did all her work anyway.

"That's nice of him. He hasn't seen any of my work so I'm not sure why he thinks that."

She raised her chin, sticking her nose in the air. "I've

assured him you will work on it, but I'll be taking the lead, as I always do."

More like taking the credit.

"What does he want?"

"He's moving into new offices. The place needs redecorating—reception area, offices, the lot. It's been planned for a while, but he's just decided to move on with it."

"Is that the gorgeous older man we saw this morning?"

I glared at Tamara as she spoke, and she clamped her lips together. Too late.

"Yes. He asked where I was working and I told him. I didn't expect anything else."

"I've got a meeting with him this afternoon. It sounds like a lot of work." Renee cast her eye over what I was working on. "That's due by close-of-business today. I hope it's going to be ready."

"Should be."

She rolled her eyes. "Get something in on time, for once in your life."

I took deep breaths, resisting the overwhelming urge to just get up and punch her in the face. I'll admit, I'd gotten into the habit of being late to hand in projects, but it was usually because I would stop and help Tamara. She was less experienced, and it wasn't like her boss would ever deign to help her.

"I'll try my best." I said it as cheerily as I could, as it would only irritate her.

Sure enough, she walked around me and toward her office. "Do that." She didn't look back as she shut the door.

I shifted my gaze from her office back to Tamara.

"So Mr Friend's Father is bringing in some business. Guess he must have appreciated what he saw too," she said.

"Oh, stop it."

"There's nothing wrong with ogling a good-looking man."

I shrugged. "Just seems wrong. I've known Rebecca since high school."

A sly smile crept across her face. "You're a grown-up now."

RIGHT BEFORE FIVE, I knocked on Renee's door.

"Enter," she called.

I blew out a breath and pushed the door open, stepping into her luxurious office. Seeing this room made me think of Cinderella for some reason. The wicked stepmother living the life of luxury while Cinderella worked in the dirt.

The room was all dark colours. Despite the ample natural light that could have come through the windows, Renee had big, heavy shades which cut it all out, and she sat in the artificial fluorescent glow I hated. She must have decorated this years before I got there; it hadn't been touched in that time. It wouldn't have surprised me to find it was the last thing she designed for herself. It was dark, just like her soul.

"I thought you would want this before I left. I've emailed you the computer files, but here's the paper version." She liked us using computer software to create designs for rooms. I'd learned to use it, but there was nothing like good, old-fashioned pen and paper to get me started.

"Leave it on the desk. I'll look it over tonight."

I nodded, dropping the file on the edge of her desk and turning.

"This Wallace Finance job could be big. It might not just be the main company. He has several subsidiaries."

I turned back and looked over my shoulder at her. "His daughter runs one of them."

She smiled, that wicked stepmother smile. "I look forward to the challenge."

"She's very protective of him." Despite their differences, I knew that to be the truth. If Rebecca got involved in this project, Renee would get away with nothing.

"Well, she has nothing to worry about. I'm sure we'll do a fine job of her father's project."

"I'm sure." *Because I'll be doing it.*

"I didn't realise how attractive he was. Such a nice man, too."

I nodded and closed the door, engulfed by the fierce protectiveness I felt for both Rebecca and her father. I'd seen Renee flirt with clients, and it grossed me out. The thought of her flirting with Neil Wallace made me sick to the stomach.

Surely he had to see through her.

TWO

A WEEK LATER, I sifted through the photos Renee had taken of the new Wallace Finance offices for the umpteenth time. They seemed to be quite spacious. It wasn't always easy to see from a photograph, but my boss refused to take me or Tamara on site to get a feel for the place. It made the whole thing quite difficult.

She hadn't sorted them, just copied them from the camera, and I couldn't help but notice she'd captured a few with Neil Wallace in them. He was always half in shot, and pointing, so I assumed he had no idea he'd managed to have his photo taken. He really was good-looking for a guy his age.

What age would he be, though? Rebecca was thirty; the same age as me. He must be maybe fifty-five or even sixty. Not bad for an older guy.

Lost in a daydream, I jumped as Tamara leaned over my shoulder.

"Ohhh there's that guy. He's very distinguished." She

walked around and sat down at her desk. "Think Renee's going to do him?"

"I hope not. Maybe I'll warn Rebecca."

She laughed. "What colours are you thinking?"

I looked back at the photo. "Cool, clean, professional. There are windows down one side of the building and they're facing east so the place will get plenty of sun. Maybe a coloured feature wall for the reception area."

"It'd help if you could see the building up close."

I rolled my eyes. "As if that's going to happen."

In the past week, I'd put together some preliminary sketches and had some colour samples that I'd gathered. Tomorrow, however, was the weekend and it was time to go home to my little flat and eat noodles while watching something mind-numbing on television.

I packed up my things. My work usually travelled with me, in case I found some inspiration. The bus ride home would take a while, and sometimes I'd see things in passing that would give me ideas.

I had a car, a Peugeot hatchback I'd found cheap at an auction site. It did the job, but the cost of petrol meant it stayed in the garage as much as possible. So, bus it was.

The bus smelled of urine, and I sat as close to the front as I could to minimise my discomfort. The bus driver seemed blissfully unaware, cranking out a song as we trundled along the bus lanes.

My pocket vibrated as my phone rang, and I fished it out to look at the screen. I didn't recognise the number and not answering crossed my mind, but given that I had about an hour-long bus ride, even a phone survey might be interesting to do.

"Hello?"

"Nicola?" The velvet voice that came down the phone sent a tingle up my spine. I might not have worked out who it was if I hadn't spoken to him so recently.

"Mr Wallace?"

"Given how long we've known each other, I think you should call me Neil." My heart pounded. How did he have this effect on me? I didn't know whether to be embarrassed or embrace it.

"Fine. Neil." I laughed.

"I was wondering what you were doing this evening?" *Oh holy shit.*

"I'm just on my way home. It's been a really long day."

"I bet. I'm told you've been working hard with Renee, designing the new look for my offices. I thought we could catch up and you could show me what you've done. You know, off the record."

The grin on my face made it ache as he spoke. I guessed I could take the car out for a drive.

"Sounds good. I ... We had some really cool ideas. Where do you want to meet?"

He paused. "Actually, I'm outside your place now."

What? How?

"I didn't know you knew where I lived."

"You're in the phone directory. That's where I got your mobile number, too."

I grinned again before my surroundings hit me. "I'm not going to be home for maybe another hour."

"Oh. Stuck in traffic?"

"On the bus."

He was smiling—I heard it in his voice. "Serves me right for rushing over."

Rushing. "Sorry. If you've got other things to do, maybe we could always do it another day?"

"I can wait."

"See you in about an hour, then." My head spun with possibilities. It shouldn't have excited me to think of him waiting for me, but it did.

"See you then."

I hung up the phone, placing it back in my pocket. He had been so polite and professional in the office. This was so confusing. I'd never had any other customer track me to my home. But then, he wasn't just any customer.

The bus stopped at the end of my street, and I slipped off my shoes, jogging the short distance to the apartment block. Neil stood outside, the jacket and tie he usually wore discarded in the warm evening. He grinned as I drew closer.

"In a hurry?"

"I didn't want to keep you waiting. Have you been outside this whole time?"

He laughed. "No. I sat in the car for a while, but I've been in meetings on and off all day and got sick of sitting down."

"Fair enough."

I pushed open the front door and led him to the elevators, pressing the up button and waiting.

"I've been working on your designs today. I've got a bit done—enough for you to get an idea of some of it."

"That sounds great. I bought this." He held up a bottle of red wine.

"I'll make some food. Have you had dinner yet?"

"We could always order pizza."

I laughed at the idea of the big businessman eating pizza in my tiny flat. I bet he'd never been on any dates like this before.

What are you doing? This isn't a date.

The elevator finally arrived, and I stole glances at him as we rose through the floors. In all the years I'd been going to Rebecca's place, I remembered him as a serious man, not seeming to have a lot of time for his daughter. Now he smiled warmly, and he seemed relaxed and happy.

We walked from the lift to my door and I slid the key into the lock, turning the handle and pushing it open.

My apartment was small, and I didn't keep a lot of things there, so at least it was tidy for visitors. My last place had been bigger, and I'd left a lot in storage at Mum and Dad's to avoid being crowded.

"I've got some red wine glasses. I just need to grab them," I said.

When I returned, Neil stood in my small living room, looking around. I smiled, taking a seat on the couch and placing the glasses and a corkscrew on the table. "It's small, but it's home."

He shrugged. "When I started my career, I lived somewhere like this for a while."

"So there's hope for me yet? I've seen the size of your house."

He laughed, sitting beside me, and I sucked in a breath at

his closeness. Not that there was much choice. To save space, I only had a two-seater couch.

While I pulled my work folder out of my bag, he opened the wine, pouring two generous glasses. "How's work going? Renee seems very full on."

I rolled my eyes. "I think that's a bit of an understatement."

Neil pushed my wine glass toward me. "Have a drink then. I doubt anyone has ever said no to her."

"I kind of get that impression. I don't want to speak ill of my boss, especially when you're doing business with her, but I think she was quite looking forward to flirting with you."

His eyebrows twitched as I said it, and I grinned without thinking about it. That made him nervous; I could see it in his face. "Thanks for the warning."

"I don't usually get the chance to warn clients, but I'll look out for you and Rebecca."

He took a sip of his wine, and I laid out the sketches I'd made, placing the colour samples down to the side. "There you go."

He was quiet, and I flicked glances between him and the papers in front of him. The man had the perfect poker face. Impossible to read.

"So?" I asked, breaking the silence.

"I like it. The feature wall is a bit bright for my taste, but it'll grow on me, I'm sure."

"This is just the preliminary idea based on the photos. I'm glad you're here to see them. It'll be easier to work through them having you to consult."

His gaze shifted back to my face, and it was so intense, I

fought the urge to look away. "I don't dislike it. Whatever you need to finish your design, it's yours."

"I appreciate it. I'm sure Renee will let you know what she needs." I winked and nudged his arm in jest.

"I'm not talking about Renee."

I gulped, and wriggled in my seat just to break the tension. "I'll be fine. Just tell me what changes you want made and I'll make them."

"Has your boss seen these?"

I nodded. "She asked for them late this afternoon. Please don't tell her you've seen them. She'll have a hissy fit."

He nodded. "Of course. It goes without saying. So, when do you need to visit the office to take a look around?" he asked, and took another sip of wine.

"I don't. That's not how Renee works."

His brows knitted together as he frowned. "How do you get a feel for the place?"

"She takes about a million photos."

"Surely that shows you what it looks like, but how do you know how big the space is? Wouldn't it matter?"

I shrugged. "It would help a lot, but that's not the way she does things."

A sly smile crept across his face. "Why don't we go?"

"Go where?"

"My offices. Bring your designs and you can see for yourself."

"When?"

He licked his lips slowly, narrowing his eyes as if scrutinising my reaction. "Now?"

I laughed, shaking my head. "I only just got home."

"So? We'll order pizza when we get there."

Some nagging part of my brain told me to hold back, to not go, that the attraction I felt for him would only bite me in the arse. The naughty side of me, the side that wanted more from this smart, attractive man, told me to follow my heart. Even if he was only being friendly.

"Okay."

He grinned, placing his glass back on the coffee table. "It's not too far from here. Come on."

"Sure." I couldn't help but smile. He stood, holding out his hand for me to take. I paused for a moment before placing my hand in his. His touch was firm and warm, and I took my time as he pulled me to my feet. I picked up my bag from beside the couch. "Are you really sure about this?"

"It's my building, and I want nothing but the best. As far as I'm concerned, you are the best, so you get whatever you need to complete the job." He had this devilish grin on his face, and a twinkle in his eyes. There was just no saying no to him like this.

"Okay," I said.

I let him lead the way, down in the elevator and to his car in the street. I shook off the increasing feeling of this being a date. *That's ridiculous.*

The late-model Audi he drove was shiny on the outside, and the soft leather seats inside almost made me moan as I sank into the passenger's side. I froze as he sat beside me, not wanting to touch anything in case I broke something, despite being curious about all the buttons on the dash.

"This is such a beautiful car," I said.

"I just got it a few days ago. I'm still getting a feel for it."

"I could go to sleep in this seat."

He laughed, starting the engine, which purred as he put it into drive and moved out and onto the street. "Don't go to sleep too quickly. It's not that long a drive."

I lost track of the time as we wove through the streets. It had been so long since I'd been in a nice car. Mine usually sat in the garage until I had to get it out, usually for my once-a-month lunch with the girls. It wasn't that great, but it looked okay.

"Still with me?" he asked as we slowed outside a huge, soft-lit building.

"Only just."

He pulled into a car park right out front and switched off the engine. "We're here. Come and take a look."

It was even more impressive than the pictures, with large glass windows facing out toward the car park. Planter boxes had already been placed in a row along the concrete path in front. If it were up to me, I'd put in flowers that would bloom big and bright, bringing life to the swanky offices. The thought made me smile.

One of the things I hated about living in an apartment was there was no room to spread my wings and decorate the way I wanted. Getting my hands on projects like this stirred the thrill, the buzz I got from the creativity found in colours and textures. I itched to get my hands dirty.

"What do you think?" he asked as he opened my door.

"It's big. So much potential."

"That's what I like to hear."

If only every job was this easy.

He plucked his mobile from his pocket and dialled. "What kind of pizza do you want?"

I shrugged. "I'm not fussed. Whatever."

"Decisive then?" There was a teasing tone in his voice.

"Meat, sauce and fat. That's all we need. I've got some cash in my purse."

Neil shook his head, directing his attention to the phone. "Hi, I'd like to order a delivery ..."

I turned away to look at the huge expanse. This room was far bigger than Renee's photos portrayed, and all the previous designs I'd created for her flashed through my mind. How many didn't look quite right because of the scale? How much more could I have done if I'd got this opportunity for every customer? What a screwed up way to run a business.

One day, when I was in business for myself I'd go out on site and look at every wall, every room and get the feel, not just the look. So much potential was wasted all because Renee wanted to claim credit for everything.

I'd seen her designs from years before, and they weren't that bad. As time moved on and designs changed, she stagnated and got left in this bad situation of her own making. Anything she designed would look dated now.

"Meatlovers with barbecue sauce. I also got chips, garlic bread, and two cans of soft drink, seeing as we left the wine at your place." Neil's voice broke through my imaginings.

"Sounds good."

"Is this helping?" He stood right behind me now, his warmth radiating against my back. It was too close for comfort, but I wasn't about to make him move away.

"Very much so. I had no idea how big the rooms were.

Getting the dimensions is one thing, seeing each room gives those dimensions meaning."

"I'm glad it helps." He stepped around me, pointing to his right. "The offices are down that way. While my office ..." he pointed to his left, "is right there."

"It's late in the project to get in an interior designer."

He twisted his mouth, a sheepish look crossing his face. "I had two come through and give me very different designs, neither of which I liked. I want something that looks modern, but still retains some traditional aspects. I'm not about to paint my reception area hot pink."

I rolled my eyes. "Caught me out. That was exactly what I was going to suggest."

He laughed, his infectious grin making me smile in response. "I might even consider it if *you* suggest it."

"Really?" No way was I going to believe that.

"No."

I caught my breath at that look in his eyes. *He's being nice to you because you're Rebecca's friend.* I had to keep remembering that.

"Lucky I'm not a fan of hot pink."

Neil wiped the back of his hand across his forehead. "Phew."

"Bright orange on the other hand ..." I raised my index finger to my mouth as if thinking while I looked around the walls.

"Don't you dare." He was so close, and his gaze focused on me. The intensity of it made my heart beat faster, and I bit down on my bottom lip to stop myself from losing my nerve as I gazed back. Memories of him looking at Rebecca with a mix of sadness and anger came flooding into my mind. She was the one who broke all of the rules, and while it would infuriate him, there was always still that touch of melancholy about him. I hadn't seen it at the time, but now the man was right in front of me and I saw the difference. He was happy.

"I'm sure we can come to some agreement."

Our moment broke as a sudden tapping on the window made me jump, and I turned to see the pizza car parked outside, the teenage delivery person pointing at the pizza.

"Looks like dinner has arrived." Neil patted my arm as he passed, and I watched as he collected the food and smiled at me on his way back in.

We sat in the middle of the room and he opened the box, spreading the chips and garlic bread out in the top half. "The workmen will wonder why this place smells of pizza first thing in the morning."

Laughing, I picked up a slice of pizza. "Their loss. I'm so hungry I think I could eat this whole thing."

Neil shook his head. "Make sure you leave some for me."

As we sat and ate our dinner, my mind raced with decorating ideas. This place would be something special—it would grow from the depths of my creative being.

It didn't matter that Renee would try to take the credit. Neil would know the truth.

Right now, that was all that mattered to me.

THREE

I BUCKLED DOWN AT WORK. Over the next week my plans took shape, aided by seeing the workspace. This had to be special for Neil.

Seven days after we'd visited the building, my mobile buzzed and I picked it up, smiling at the message.

> I've just been given two tickets to a comedy show for tonight.
> Interested?

I stared at Neil's text. This was a fascinating development.

> I'd love to. What time?

I decided to throw caution to the wind and go out with him.

My heart sang at the thought of spending time with him. I hadn't been out in the evening in forever, spending most of my time concentrating on work.

I laughed. The pizza hadn't been that bad. It wasn't something I ate very often, and it had suited the evening.

My wardrobe was a mess, and when I got home I went straight to work finding something suitable for a night out.

I pulled everything out to go through, and clothing lay scattered over the bed and floor. I made a mental note to clean up at the weekend. Sometimes I scavenged around used clothing stores to find bargains and brought back all manner of things, some of which I'd never worn. It had to be time for a sort-out.

Hidden down the back of the wardrobe was a bag of clothing and I opened it, smiling as I dug out a red dress, knee-length with a halter-neck top. It was a bit dressy, but still fine for casual wear.

As I draped it over me, it seemed a little baggy. More than likely I'd lost weight since I'd bought it, but somewhere in that wardrobe were a couple of belts. God, was I falling back into old habits? My relationship with food had always been a struggle.

I found one buried under a pile of shoes, and slipping the black leather around my waist, I smiled as I looked in the mirror. There must be so many things hidden in there that I could wear to work such as this, instead of the clothes I'd gotten into a routine with. *Time for a change.*

I checked the time. It had taken me forty-five minutes to pull apart the wardrobe and find something. I had fifteen minutes to check my makeup and pull myself together before Neil arrived.

On the dot of seven p.m. there was a tap on the door, and I ran before stopping myself.

Don't look too eager.

I opened the door to a large smile on his face. He'd been home to change too at a guess, his business clothes discarded for a polo shirt and jeans. A flush crept up my cheeks; I was clearly overdressed.

"Ready to go?" he asked.

"Sure, I'll just grab my bag."

If he thought I'd overdone it, he didn't say a word. "There's a steakhouse just down the road from the theatre. I've been meaning to try it for a while."

"Sounds great." He waited outside the door as I grabbed my bag, and I walked out the door and past him, turning to close and lock my apartment.

He cast his eyes over me. "You look lovely. I hope you didn't go to any huge effort for me."

I shook my head. "Oh, I just grabbed something from my wardrobe."

"It looks good. Shall we?"

I linked my arm in his and we walked toward the lift. Tapping my foot impatiently as we waited, his presence was comforting, the situation nerve-wracking.

Maybe I was reading too much into this, but I liked the idea of spending more time with him.

We stood in silence, and I breathed a sigh of relief when the lift bell rang out. Stepping into the elevator, he squeezed my arm in his.

"A friend of mine is the theatre owner. We were discussing business today when he gave me these tickets. No idea what this is going to be like. It's part of a comedy festival."

I grinned. "It can't be too bad."

Neil shrugged. "If it is, we can always sneak out and go for a drink somewhere."

The lift doors opened and we strolled out to the car, with him opening my door as he had the week before.

The bright lights of the city filled me with excitement. I'd spent so many nights hidden away in my little apartment, not venturing out. After a twenty minute drive, we left the car in a nearby parking building and strode down the street. It was a warm night, and Neil took my hand in his as he led me to the restaurant.

The steakhouse was busy, and the smell of roasting meat left my mouth watering. The diners were dressed in a mix of casual and dressy clothes. My outfit hadn't been a bad choice after all. Neil and I would fit in nicely.

"Do you have a table for two?" Neil asked.

"Come this way." The waitress smiled as she picked up the menu and led us to an empty table.

In the centre of the room, flames flared as the steaks cooked. My stomach grumbled and I sat down, grinning at the show put on by the chef as he flipped the food. Loud sizzles filled the air alongside laughter and the sound of the customers chatting. This place was so full of life, and it was contagious.

"What do you think?" Neil asked.

"It all smells amazing."

He ran his finger down the menu. "There's every type of steak you can think of, and ..." Neil looked around. "The salad bar is over there."

"What are you going to get?" I asked.

"I think I'm going to go with the eye fillet. Might as well jump in at the deep end." He passed me over the menu with a smile.

My eyes nearly popped out of their sockets at the prices listed. "You must really like steak to spend that much." I laughed.

"No more than any other food. I just think we should make the most of having a night out. Pick whatever you want. I'm paying."

The way he smiled was so genuine. For financial reasons I was used to restraint, and while the prices weren't as much as the place I had a monthly lunch at with my friends, guilt gripped me. Despite his words, I didn't want to look too greedy.

"The rump steak will be fine."

He narrowed his eyes. "Are you sure?"

"Perfectly." I smiled, placing the menu back on the table.

He looked up, and must have made eye contact with the waitress who came over to the table.

"Are you ready to order?"

"Yes," I said.

"Two eye fillet steaks please." Neil didn't take his eyes off me, and I raised my brows at him.

"Are you eating two?" I asked, resisting letting go of a grin.

"One for me, one for you. Don't think you're getting away with ordering a cheaper cut of meat."

I laughed. "I'm happy with whatever."

The waitress stood there, flicking glances between the two of us. "Anything to drink?"

"Whatever Mr Wallace wants." I smiled sweetly.

His eyes danced with mischief. "Bubbles or still wine?"

"Still white please."

He cast his gaze over the menu again. "A bottle of the Riesling, please."

The waitress nodded. "How would you like your steaks cooked?"

"Medium rare." We spoke at the same time, and I broke down in giggles as Neil shook his head.

"The salad bar is just over there. Help yourselves." The waitress picked up the menu.

"You're bossy," I said.

"I told you. I'm making the most of a night on the town. I don't get out much."

"Oh you poor thing. Mind you, neither do I."

Neil leaned back in his chair. "I don't understand why. I

thought you'd have men falling over themselves to take you out."

I did get asked out from time to time, but in general, I'd kept to myself the past three years. Burned out by previous relationships, I'd smiled and laughed with my friends as they'd talked about their conquests, but most nights my own company was all I needed. "I'm not much of a social butterfly."

He said nothing for what felt like the longest time and nodded. "I understand the need to spend time alone. Don't get me wrong, I enjoy a good night out, but there's a lot to be said for an evening by yourself in front of the television."

The waitress returned, placing two glasses on the table. Neil nodded, as she poured the wine.

I nodded. "I love living by myself. I get to choose when I socialise without having to deal with roommates." Sipping my wine, I smiled. "I had enough of sharing. When I was at university, I lived with a girl who had zero idea about privacy. We had one of those glass-walled showers. I'd be in the shower, completely naked, and she'd come in to use the toilet without even knocking. Drove me insane."

Neil had just taken a sip of wine, and coughed, turning a little red.

"Are you okay?" I asked.

"That was some mental image." He laughed.

My cheeks burned with embarrassment, but I chuckled. "I think I should go and get some salad. Might stop me from babbling."

"Yes, we should get salad, but don't let it stop you from talking. I enjoy listening."

My face went nuclear hot and I stood, rather than sit there melting into the seat. It didn't take much to get me flustered around him, but at the same time, he was just so easy to talk to. I'd have to be careful not to accidentally reveal any of Rebecca's secrets.

With plates full of salad, we returned to the table just in time for the steaks to arrive. I didn't know how Neil felt, but I was ravenous.

"Would you like some sauce?" The waitress held a tray with so many choices. I selected the peppercorn, even though I craved the garlic. I'd avoid the inevitable bad breath it would leave behind, even if it would no doubt taste divine.

I cut in and the steak was cooked to perfection, nice and pink on the inside. It sliced like a hot knife through butter, and I salivated as I raised the fork for the first bite. It was every bit as good as it smelled. I'd savour this memory next time I sat at the very expensive Le Grande restaurant and ordered salad.

The avoidance of conversation was easy as both of us tucked into our beautiful meals. I ate until I felt bloated, leaning back in my chair.

"How's your steak?" he asked.

"Wonderful. It just melts in the mouth." I hadn't had a steak like this in forever. I'd been so entrenched in my light, cheap diet.

"Mine too. I should have checked this place out a long time ago. It's amazing." He waggled his eyebrows, and I couldn't help but grin. "I think a return visit is definitely in order."

"I don't know if I can eat all this." I let out a loud sigh, placing my hand over my stomach.

"I know the feeling." He looked at his watch. "The show starts in about twenty minutes. I'll grab the bill and we'll get out of here."

Before I could stop it, I burped, loud and not so proud, as I covered my mouth with my hand. Horrified, I grabbed my glass and took a drink only for Neil to chuckle.

"That good, huh?"

"Must have been." I laughed and got to my feet.

"If we go now, we'll be seated in plenty of time. If you're good, I'll buy you an ice cream or something."

That made me laugh even harder. "If I'm good at what?"

"The night is full of possibilities, Miss Crandell."

His eyes flashed with mischief again, yet he made me feel safe when I was with him.

WE SAT down for the show. The seats weren't too bad; we had a good view of the stage. One after another, comedians came out and I laughed until I cried. The whole time Neil sat next to me, laughing just as hard. At intermission, he even bought me the promised ice cream.

The drive home was quiet, relaxed. My head was on a high from the fun of the evening, and the company. Unable to shake the feeling that this was a date, I ached for more.

"Have fun?" Neil asked.

"It was amazing. Thank you so much for inviting me. I don't think I've laughed so much in a long time."

"Me either. I'm glad you could come."

I studied his profile for the longest time. Was this a date for him, or just a nice evening out with a friend? I licked my lips, and tested the water. "Did you think about inviting Rebecca? I think she would have enjoyed it."

Neil sighed. "Rebecca and I don't really have the kind of relationship where we do this kind of thing together."

"Why not?"

He shrugged. "It's just never been like that between us."

"But you thought I might like it."

Neil wriggled in his chair, not seeming comfortable, but I wanted to know what was going through his head. I didn't want to let this go. "You have a great sense of humour, and you're fun to be around. Things with Rebecca can be a bit awkward. It's easier sometimes to just leave it be."

My heart broke a little when he said the words. I might not have gone out with my father, but he lived out of town. Neil was right there, and there was a gap between him and Rebecca that shouldn't have existed.

If I spent more time with him, maybe I could help him heal that void.

Would he let me in?

FOUR

AFTER THAT, Neil was a regular face to my little apartment, approving designs before Renee even saw them and encouraging me more than anyone had in forever.

"Do you get to see your parents often?" he asked. It was three weeks since our first trip to the offices, and we were sitting with all my design pages spread across the floor. He'd stopped for Chinese food on the way to my place, and I had just taken the biggest mouthful of Sweet and Sour Pork.

I'd never eaten so much takeaway food in my life.

"Not as much as I'd like to. They live a bit out of town, and I don't know if I trust my car to travel that far on a regular basis." I spooned some more food onto my plate.

"Is it that bad?"

I shook my head. "Not really. Just needs a decent service. I get out to see them when I can."

"I saw them last weekend."

Confused, I put my fork down. "You went to see them?"

Neil grinned. "I commissioned your father for a painting for the foyer. I thought it was fitting, given you were doing the rest of the work."

To say I was touched was an understatement. I knew how pricey Dad's paintings could be, and while I knew Neil would be doing it to say he had a Robert Crandell original, that he'd thought of me warmed my heart. "That's very good of you."

"I know a good investment when I see one." He shot me a flirty smile, or was it? He either had to be the hardest person to read, or I had completely misinterpreted his interest. Was this all just because I was Rebecca's friend, or was his sudden interest in spending time with me related to work or pleasure?

Whatever it was, I grew more reluctant for him to go at the end of the evening, but I'd never been one to throw myself at someone, and in this particular case risk complete and utter humiliation.

"I told them I'd hired your firm to do the rest of the work. They seemed pleased, but your father doesn't think you're making the most of your talents."

"You talked to them about me?"

He shrugged. "Only as far as to say that I was very impressed with your work and glad I ran into you. I didn't tell them about my visiting you so often; I don't know if they'd understand."

They wouldn't understand? I didn't understand. "What wouldn't they understand?"

I'd never seen Neil blush, but the pink tinge to his cheeks left me even more confused. "I thought they might think there was more to it than just you working on my building."

Is there?

I couldn't speak, couldn't bring myself to ask the question on the tip of my tongue. I tried to read his face, but that proved impossible. My heart raced when I was near him, and his gentle and kind manner stirred me in a way I hadn't experienced for a long time. My previous boyfriends had been younger, brasher. Maybe age brought experience and a manner that wasn't in the types of guys I usually went for.

Whatever it was, I wanted this project to drag on for as long as possible so that these visits would continue.

"I still have to go back and visit again once he's finished. Do you think I should tell them I've spent a lot of evenings at your place lately?" His gaze was fixed on me, and whatever blush he'd had was gone from his cheeks. The intensity coming from him scared the crap out of me.

"I don't know if that's such a good idea."

He leaned closer. "I didn't think it would be. I don't want them thinking my visits are something that they're not."

So, what are they? I wanted to ask the question so bad, but the answer could have been as simple as him wanting to oversee his project, and I might make a complete idiot of myself.

He leaned a little closer again, and I gulped. Talk about mixed messages. Was he as confused as I was? I licked my lips, looking at his that were so close. What would he be like to kiss? This was so wrong, but I'd never wanted anyone as much as I wanted him in that moment.

Instead I nodded, and he pulled away, the moment lost.

If there ever was a moment to begin with.

"I'll leave the leftovers here as usual. I'm sure they'll make a good lunch for tomorrow." He smiled.

And as he stood and made his way to the door, I was left wondering if in his own way he was taking care of me, like someone did for a person they loved. My imagination raced with possibilities, but then again, given Neil's daughter's relationship with me, perhaps it was just a friendly gesture.

My heart had already become entangled in these feelings that I couldn't control. I'd tried to resist, but he was so special. Were there other women he'd spent evenings with like this that he hadn't been dating?

So many questions, and yet, my mouth remained closed. The last thing I needed was to make a fool of myself.

I'd had enough of that in my life.

THE FOLLOWING EVENING, I was home alone, sitting in the quiet, still thinking about the night before. I hadn't heard from Neil since last night, which wasn't unusual, but the day had a hollow feeling about it. *I miss him.*

I jumped as the phone rang loudly beside me.

I sighed, picking it up.

"Hello?"

"Nicola." My mother's soft voice echoed down the line. Given that they were in the middle of nowhere, they had nothing but a basic phone service that buzzed at times from nearby electric fences. There were times when the echo was so bad, it was as if she'd called me from the bottom of a well.

"Hi, Mum."

"I just wanted to see how you were. Rebecca's father came to see us the other day. He told us you were doing some work for him. He commissioned your father to paint a landscape for him."

I smiled. "Mr Wallace told me."

"He says you're doing a wonderful job. We were so proud to hear him sing your praises. How is work? Is that horrible woman any nicer?"

Hearing my mother's voice and the words brought tears to my eyes. I'd never get sick of hearing how proud my parents were of me. Sometimes it was the only solace I had when things went bad in my life.

"Renee's the same. At least with this job she can't claim all of the credit."

"I don't know why you don't go out on your own."

"It's a big jump out of my comfort zone. You know how I feel about those."

Mum laughed. "Says the most adventurous girl I know. As long as you're happy."

I closed my eyes. All my recent happy memories involved Neil. Maybe we hadn't gone down the romantic track I dreamed of, but we were friends at least.

"I'm getting there."

"Good. What else have you been doing?"

I sighed. "Work. I've got lunch with the girls tomorrow, so that should be nice. Nothing ever changes much."

"How are they?"

"Oh, you know. Katya is a continuous pain in the butt, wanting to get everything perfect for her wedding. She keeps calling me for colour advice. Gemma is working on some modelling job, and Rebecca ..." *I've got feelings for Rebecca's father and she has no idea.* "I don't know what Rebecca's up to. I'll see her tomorrow at lunch."

Rebecca had acted odd at the last lunch. She'd rejected the salad we all usually ate and had eaten the most delectable, tender steak I think I'd ever seen. It had been a long time since I'd bought something like that, and the thought of it even a month later made my mouth water.

The steak was three times the price of the salad, so reluctantly, I'd tucked into my salad, following our boring tradition. I always considered myself lucky that it was what the others wanted to eat too—it was the cheapest thing on a very expensive menu.

"Met anyone special?"

That was my mother's way of asking if I had a boyfriend again. I hadn't had a serious relationship in what felt like forever. It had been three years since my heart had been broken by Shaun. To be fair, we broke each other.

I would never forget the sorrow in his eyes when the doctor told us that the way I had abused my body over the years was most likely the cause of my failure to fall pregnant. We'd had it all—the apartment together, the happy life—but when I was told at the age of twenty-seven that my urge to be as thin as I could to look good was the likely cause of me not being able to carry the baby I craved, it all fell apart.

Shaun said he didn't blame me, but I could see it in his eyes. Life with him hadn't helped my eating issues at all. He'd loved the way I looked at my thinnest, even when my friends voiced their concerns. At least, that was how it'd seemed.

"I don't know. I don't get out as much as I used to."

"I hate thinking of you being alone. Come and see us soon."

I nodded. "I will. Promise."

"I got some more chickens last weekend. Your father says I've got far too many, but the eggs are selling so well down at the market. It's all that space I've given them, they've been able to run free and it shows in the food."

I bit down on my bottom lip, imagining those chickens running around and Mum following them. I stifled a laugh. Calls like this made me homesick. What I wouldn't do to go there now, breathe in the fresh air, and even feed those damn chickens. Dad would be painting in his studio, and the number of half-finished sculptures in the back yard would have increased as Mum found inspiration and then got bored with it.

One day when I had my own home, I'd have something in the yard from her, and a painting in the house from him.

When Shaun and I had broken up, I'd crawled home to them for a while before taking up the job with Renee. There had been times in the past three years that had left me wishing I'd stayed on the farm, but that wouldn't have helped me move forward.

I lay down on the couch, cradling my phone to my ear. "Sounds good, Mum. I hope you're getting good money from the eggs."

"I'm making more on those than I have from my artwork for a while. Thank goodness your father's in demand."

"Glad to hear it."

Closing my eyes, I did my best to listen to my mother talking about what she and Dad had been doing. I missed them desperately at times, and simply the sound of her voice was soothing. It wouldn't be the first time I'd fallen asleep on the phone to her; I'd done it before, safe and secure with Mum at the other end of the line.

What would they think of Neil's visits to my apartment?

Drowsiness overtook me, and I went to sleep with thoughts of Neil in my apartment on my mind. I couldn't get enough of his company. It was soothing, but not in a parental kind of way which took me by surprise, but felt so normal at the same time.

Being with him excited me far more than it should.

FIVE

ON THE LAST Friday of every month, I would take the afternoon off and have an extended lunch break with my friends. Today was catch-up day.

The last time we were at Le Grande, the restaurant we traditionally went to, things hadn't quite gone as they usually did. Normal fare was to eat our salads, catch up on gossip, and part ways. I usually saw Katya during the month and sometimes Gemma, Rebecca very rarely. After our last encounter, it would be good to see her again.

Katya and Gemma were already at the table when I got there, with Rebecca last, as usual. When she arrived, I couldn't stop glancing at her. *Does she know about her father's visits to me?*

"So ..." Gemma started. "Last time we were here, there was a gorgeous guy washing cars across the road and he knew you. Are you going to spill the beans?"

The question was directed at Rebecca, who shrugged.

Gemma was right; the guy had been hot. At a guess, six foot with beautiful abs, and he'd waved at Rebecca and called to her like some kind of lunatic.

"He's my neighbour," she said.

"Can you introduce me?" Gemma asked.

Rebecca's eyes flashed with irritation, but she smiled as sweetly as I'd ever seen. "He's taken. His girlfriend is lovely."

Gemma scowled. "The good ones always are."

Somehow, Gemma and Katya missed the undertone coming from Rebecca. While they started talking about Katya's wedding plans, I kept my eye on my mysterious friend. Something was different about her. Was I not the only one keeping secrets? We'd sat in this restaurant once a month for years, and despite us not being as close as we had been in the past, we still shared our intimacies.

She yawned, and locked gazes with me. "How about you?" she asked. "How have you been?"

"Work is busy. I'm glad to have an afternoon off."

Rebecca laughed. "Tell me about it. It's a nice lead-in to the weekend at least."

"Are you ready to order?" The waiter stood over us.

"I'd like the salad," I said, pointing to the menu.

"I want that big, fatty steak I had last time. Then I'm going to go home and sleep it off." Rebecca winked at me, and I rechecked the menu to see what the price was. It sounded so good, but I couldn't justify the expense. I sighed, and smiled as the waiter moved around the table.

Rebecca nudged me. "You should try it. It helped break me out of the funk I was in."

I shook my head. "I'm watching my weight."

Her brows furrowed. "I think you do that way too much. You're gorgeous, Nicola. You don't have to get even thinner."

"Can we talk about something else?"

"I worry about you."

I bit down on my lower lip hard as she slipped her arm around my shoulders. I knew she meant well, and I knew she thought I was shallow, but the reality was that while I'd fought my issues around how I looked, I just couldn't afford the meal she was having.

"I'm fine. It's tempting, though. I really like the salad."

She rolled her eyes. "Whatever."

I let it slide. There was no point in protesting. She could win this one.

———

"DO you want to see how it's all going?" Neil asked in the evening, over another bottle of wine and a chicken pizza. He'd come over wanting to check on a minor alteration Renee had tried to get past him. It seemed she wasn't content with letting me do my job—she wanted to make a change. I guessed so there was some truth to her claim of having completed some work on the project.

"The decorating?"

He grinned. "Yeah. It's moving along quickly. I thought you might be interested in the progress."

Excitement grew in me at the thought of seeing my work come to life. Sure, I'd visited buildings I'd designed refits for, but it was usually after the fact and out of curiosity, not part of my work. Even seeing it partially done would be thrilling.

We drove in that gorgeous soft leather–seated car to the building. My heart jumped at the sight of the half-finished work space. What I wouldn't give to spend a day with a paint roller, getting stuck into the job myself.

My small apartment didn't afford much space for me to get creative. One day I'd have a bigger place, with a room dedicated to my art. The thought made me giddy.

The interior of the building smelled of fresh paint. Large sheets of canvas covered the floor, splattered with paint, and I walked carefully across until I got to the centre of the room.

"What do you think?" Neil asked.

"It's shaping up nicely. They're a lot further along than I thought they'd be."

He laughed. "I'm paying them overtime to get it done quickly. I want out of the old building and into here now. It'll be good for everyone to be in a different environment."

Neil pointed in the direction of his office. "This is nearly finished. I even have furniture in there."

"Really? You're that far along?"

"Come and have a look."

I gasped as I walked in the door. It looked exactly as I'd pictured it in my head, a mixture of new and traditional with polished wooden furniture, including the bookcase along the wall to hold files. It was perfect.

Almost.

"What on earth is that couch? I thought we were going with dark brown or black leather." Before I could stop myself, my hands were on my hips, and I scowled at the sight of a navy fabric couch.

A guilty expression passed over Neil's face. "Renee had

trouble finding the right thing. She said microfiber would be easier to clean anyway."

"It's the wrong colour, and she's an idiot." Anger grew in me at this last-minute change. The hours I'd spent poring over my plans for this place blown by a single stupid decision. It shouldn't have got me so mad, but I had put my heart into this design.

His design.

"Nicola, it's okay. Don't get upset." Neil placed his hands on my arms.

I sniffed, raising my gaze to meet his. It was such a minor thing, but I'd worked so hard on this, and for that single piece to be out of place hurt. "I wanted it to be perfect."

His eyes searched mine, and he frowned, clearly not liking what he saw. "It is perfect."

He cared about how I felt, I saw it in his face, and without thinking, I raised my hand to his temple. As our gazes locked, I pulled my hand back, heat blazing in my cheeks. Instead of shying away from my touch he mimicked it, cupping my face in his hands and leaning over until our faces were mere inches apart.

"It's perfect," he said.

My heart thudded as I couldn't look anywhere but into those blue eyes penetrating my soul.

"Nicola," he whispered. We were locked together in space and time, neither one of us moving. My heart begged for him to kiss me; my brain fought against it.

This. Is. Rebecca's. Father.

I didn't care.

I wanted to be on the leather couch I'd envisaged for his

office, with him on top of me. Raising my hands to cover his, I lifted them from my face and slid them down to the small of my back where let them rest, my body pressed against him.

He was what I wanted. He was what I craved.

His Adam's apple bobbed as he swallowed hard. I had the same effect on him as he did on me, and I took the initiative, pressing my lips to his and tasting him for the first time. He opened his mouth, letting me make tentative touches with my tongue. His hands dropped lower, gripping my butt as the kiss intensified.

Neil wanted me. He hardened against my leg and I pressed myself tighter against him. Screw Renee and her bullshit interference. I'd have sex with him on the couch she picked and spoil the one thing she had chosen.

No.

I pulled away, pressing my hands against Neil's chest. Yes, I wanted him, but not like this. Not some piece of revenge against my boss.

"Nicola?" He seemed breathless, bewilderment lighting his face.

"If we do this now, it'll be for all the wrong reasons."

"So tell me what the right reasons are."

My mouth went dry. He gazed at me with the longing I shared, but I couldn't do it. If something was to happen between us, it couldn't be this way.

"Do you want me to replace the couch. Is that what you want?" His confusion was clear in his tone, and he pleaded with his eyes for me to answer him.

"Yes," I answered like a petulant child, finally getting the way I wanted. I didn't care about the couch—I cared that he had kissed me back and wanted me the way I wanted him.

It scared the crap out of me.

"I'll find a replacement," he said curtly. "I'll get you home now. I think we've seen all we can."

I'd wounded him, this beautiful, caring man who had spent the last few weeks showing me who he really was. All this time forming this friendship and I'd screwed it up one confusing moment.

We drove in silence back to my place. I didn't know what else to say. When I closed my eyes, I could still feel his lips on mine, how warm and soft they were. His body against mine, as turned on as I was burned in my memory.

"We're here."

He got out and walked around the car, opening my door, and I stepped out, standing before him.

"Good night, Nicola."

Last time he'd walked me to my door. Sure, it was only a few metres away, and we'd parked right outside the building, but still—he was ready to say good night here and let me go.

"I ... goodnight." I couldn't say anything more, couldn't bring myself to mention what had happened between us. Not to mention what we'd nearly done.

He stood beside the car, watching as I walked toward the apartment block. I turned at the door, and for just a moment his expression seemed so sad before he got back in and drove away.

What the hell just happened?

SIX

AFTER THREE MONTHS we were finished, from design to completed in what had seemed like record time.

The visits had stopped. There had been no point going over the plans again, not when everything had been finalised. Was that the reason he'd stopped coming to see me, or had I scared him away?

Distracted, I struggled to concentrate at work, barely paying attention to a design that was thankfully much less complex than Neil's. My heart ached with how much I missed him; my body still remembered the way I'd pressed against him.

I want him.

My desk phone buzzed and I jumped, to Tamara's amusement. I rolled my eyes at her as I picked it up.

"Nicola Crandell speaking."

"Nicola." Neil's familiar tones soothed their way down the phone line.

"Uh hi."

"I'm calling to ask if you wanted to see the completed building tonight. No pressure, but I want to show it off to the woman I know is responsible for how good it looks."

I smiled into the phone. Even if he didn't want to see me on a personal level, he still had regard for me professionally.

"Nicola?"

Shit. Smiling into the phone didn't equal sound coming out. "I'd love to."

"Want to make it the usual? I'll pick you up maybe about seven and we'll order a pizza when we get there?"

My heart soared at the simple question. Did I want to spend time with him? *Yes.*

"Sounds great. See you then."

I closed my eyes as I put down the phone, trying to get my breathing under control. The sound of his voice alone had made my body react, and I couldn't help but smile.

"Holy crap, what was that?" Tamara laughed.

"What do you mean?" I opened my eyes to see her grinning.

"What was that call about? Pretty sure you were orgasming at your desk."

I slapped my hand across my mouth, stifling a giggle. "Was not. I'm having dinner with a friend."

"A *good* friend." Her tone was teasing, but I knew she meant well.

"Maybe. We'll see." *I hope so.*

I was such a terrible person, having this longing for a man I couldn't have. Then again, he seemed to want me too. I'd never been with anyone like Neil. I'd been with nice guys before, but Neil was a gentleman, a sweet, gentle soul who seemed so in sync with me.

The rest of the day had a different vibe about it. Neil hadn't shut me out completely; maybe we could still salvage a friendship out of this.

I trundled home on the bus. Today it wasn't too bad; it was a fairly new vehicle with clean seats and shiny bars. The regular bus driver sang today's tune with a vibrancy I understood. If I hadn't been so self-conscious about how I sounded, especially when singing, I might have even joined in.

Running in the door at home, I pulled open the wardrobe to find something to wear. This might not be a date, but damn it, I wanted to look good for myself and for Neil. Would he mention the other night? Would I get the courage to bring it up?

I smiled as I spotted an old favourite dress. The dark blue brought out the lighter aqua of my eyes, and the cut was flattering without being too revealing.

On the dot of seven, I ran to the knock on the door, smiling widely as I pulled it open.

Neil took a deep breath, casting his gaze over me. He'd changed too, out of his work suit and into a polo shirt and dark-coloured slacks. Had he made an effort too?

"You look ..." He didn't finish his sentence as our eyes met —he didn't have to. His surprise and wonder were obvious.

"I thought I should put some effort in, seeing as it's all complete. I can't wait to see how it looks."

Neil straightened his expression. "It looks amazing, and I have you to thank. Ready to go?"

I nodded, picking up my purse and grabbing a cotton cardigan to go over the top of my shoulders in case I got cold.

This time, the drive was silent but not uncomfortable. I still had no idea what to say to him, how to address the kiss. Was he as confused as I was?

The planter boxes had floral bushes in them now. Come spring, they would burst into colour, bringing the outside of the building to life.

Neil and I walked to the centre of the reception area, and I cast my eye over every feature with pride. Particularly the gorgeous artwork my father had painted. I didn't know how much Neil had paid for it, and I didn't want to ask. A big part of me was grateful, as I knew how much he and Mum depended on commissions.

The painting was a landscape, and I recognised it at once as the view from Mum and Dad's house—the beautiful rolling hills, and the pale blue sky dotted with white fluffy clouds.

"I asked him for something familiar, something to link you with the work you'd done. Maybe you won't get the credit, but I know how hard you've worked on this." He spoke softly, standing close behind me. This wasn't fair. The air was electric, charged with whatever this attraction was between us. He had to feel it too.

"It's lovely. It looks great out here."

"Your father is very talented. Your mother is working on a sculpture for my garden."

I turned toward him and slapped my hand across my mouth. "It's so good of you to give them the work."

"They're good people. I hadn't seen them since you girls

all left school. They never change, though, do they?" His smile was kind and caring. I didn't dare ask if he'd done this for me, but something in the back of my head told me he had.

"No. Crazy old hippies. I need to go and see them."

"I think they'd like that."

My heart froze as I stared at him. Had he had a conversation with my parents about me? What had they discussed? Here I was, battling these errant feelings for him, and he was off chatting to my dad. My skin itched with discomfort.

"I still didn't tell them we'd been spending so much time together. Even if it's for professional reasons, I don't think they'd understand." His gaze didn't falter, and my heart went from zero to about a million. "All those evenings in your apartment probably don't look appropriate."

What should I say to that? That as much as I loved seeing the final decorating, I hated the thought of him no longer visiting? How could I keep up the contact now? I hadn't thought about this part.

"I enjoyed them." That was all I could say, and from the way his lips twitched, he would miss them too.

"So did I. What am I going to do with my evenings now?" His tone was teasing, but the words had depth. So we weren't going to discuss our kiss. "You could always accompany me to my official opening."

"Will Rebecca be there?"

He laughed. "Rebecca never attends any of these things. She'll wander into my office when it suits her ladyship, and for a little while I'll enjoy the pleasure of my daughter's company before she flits off."

I took a deep breath. "Then I accept."

A smile crossed his lips as he gazed at me. "Good. That's settled."

"Renee won't like it."

He grinned. "Do you really think I care what she thinks?"

I suppressed a smirk. "I know you don't. Troublemaker."

"Who, me?"

Oh, this was awful. He was so cute when he was being incorrigible. That sly smile of his that just screamed how naughty he was being.

I laughed. "I love the way you think, but she's still my boss."

He shrugged. "Not forever. If only her other clients could see who does the actual work."

In such a short time, he'd become my biggest defender. This man was like a knight in shining armour, except I doubted he had any intention of sweeping me off my feet. While I'd worked on his project, however, we'd at least become friends.

Even if his daughter, didn't know.

"Want to see my office again?"

I gulped. "Sure?"

When he opened the door, I saw the reason for his invitation. The navy couch was gone, and in its place was a dark brown leather sofa. I gasped as I ran my hand along the back of it, grinning at the smile on his face.

"Better?"

"It's perfect."

"I went right out the day after we looked at the office and found it. You were right; it's much better."

I drew level with him, licking my lips as I met his gaze. My heart thrummed as I lifted my hand to his chest.

"I think I should order this food." He pulled away, turning his back to me, and I flopped down on the couch in surrender, my cheeks burning with embarrassment. It didn't matter how much I wanted to feel his touch, taste his kiss. This was his way of saying he didn't want me in that way.

Stroking the leather with my fingers, I scratched the surface with my magenta-painted fingernails. The leather was soft under my fingertips, and I continued scratching it, distracted by his rejection.

Of course he didn't want me. I'd gone to school with his daughter. He didn't think anything more of me than that kid who used to spend time at their place.

His skin was warm as he placed his hand over mine, and I looked up to see a bemused expression on his face.

"I buy a new couch because you want me to, and the first thing you do is try and scratch it to pieces?"

That feeling was back. The one that made my heart soar as our gazes were locked. He seemed not to want to move his hand away from mine.

In my whole adult life, I'd never been so confused.

"I haven't forgotten what happened last time we were here. I just don't know how to process it." There was that smooth tone again, the caring one, the one that addled my brain and made me want to pull him down on top of me.

"I don't know either," I whispered.

"You kissed me. I didn't not want it." He raised his other hand and ran a finger down my cheek. "When you pulled away, I wanted to stop you."

"Why didn't you?"

"Because of who you are, who I am. Us being together could destroy everything."

I bit down on my bottom lip, blinking back tears. "I know. You want to protect Rebecca."

"And you. Your job, your life. I want you so badly, I can't breathe. It's taken me these past two weeks to recover from the feeling of you being in my arms." He turned at a loud tap on the window. "That'll be the food. Let's go and christen the lunch room table."

I stared at him from under my eyelashes as he looked back around, and smirked. "With our dinner," he clarified.

Even a suggestion of something else had me burst out laughing, and Neil walked away, shaking his head as he went to pay the driver.

I needed a moment and sat with my eyes closed, thinking over his words in my head. His confession didn't help the situation, but now at least I knew our attraction was mutual.

Standing, I made my way out to the reception area and trailed behind Neil as he led me to the lunch room.

He placed the pizza on the table and opened the box. "We don't have any crockery yet. We'll have to eat with our fingers."

"So," I said as I pulled out a slice, twisting the cheese around my fingers, "does that make this a date?"

Neil rolled his eyes. "I don't know what to call it." He sat opposite me. "I do, however, know that I want you on my arm for the opening. Not just because you designed this, but because you'll make me look good."

Revealing his feelings opened him up in a whole new way to me as he sat there with a devilish grin on his face.

"Oh, turning into a regular Mr Flirt now, aren't we?"

He laughed and took a bite out of his pizza. "Sorry, can't talk with my mouth full," he mumbled.

My cheeks flushed as I shook my head and laughed, but not from embarrassment. It wasn't just that he was attractive and kind and caring. However short our conversation had been the other night, with everything out there any sense of being uncomfortable was gone, and I could relax again.

The way it had always been between us.

"ARE YOU NUTS?" Tamara screwed up her face as she stared at me. I'd told her half the story. That Mr Wallace had invited me to his opening—not that I had all these lusty, romantic feelings for one of the last people I should ever want.

I shrugged. "Maybe. It should be a good night out."

"Renee will hate it."

I took a sip of my coffee. We were downstairs having a chocolate slice and a hit of caffeine before another great day at work.

"I've decided I don't care. What's she going to do—fire me? She needs us, Tamara, more than we need her. I used to think that this job was everything, that even though I hated working for her one day what I did would be enough. But it never will. She'll milk all our talent and make herself look better."

Tamara nodded. "That's all well and good, but who's going to pay your rent if you lose your job?"

"She can't fire me for being out with a friend, even if he is a client. I knew him well before I did the work. She can make things uncomfortable, but I could always quit and go home to Mum and Dad." I laughed.

"That's a great look at your age." She grinned, and I just knew I was alone in my little act of rebellion.

"I've fought for so long to move forward, but I'm just treading water working here. I need a reboot of my life."

She reached across the table, placing her hand over mine. "I just hope you know what you're doing."

"You know what? For the first time in my life I have no idea, and it feels wonderful."

We made our way up to the offices in that old rickety lift I wouldn't miss whenever I left this place. Cherie grimaced as we walked through, beckoning for us to draw close.

"Renee just arrived and she's in such a temper today. Giving you two a heads up."

"Thanks," Tamara said.

"Oh good." That was all I needed, and on any other day it would have filled me with a sense of doom. Today, though, my heart was dizzy over my upcoming date with Neil. Even if it wasn't a real date.

Every day I came in here and worked from eight until five. Sometimes, I didn't even take a lunch break. Today was different. Today I was hunting for the perfect dress to wear to the building opening.

I could have waited until after work and searched using

the computer at home, but this was the first day of my fight back against the evil tyranny that was Renee Jameson. That thought made me smile.

Maybe I'd take a look on a few job search sites too.

I owed myself that much.

SEVEN

IT TOOK me two days to find the perfect dress. I looked at so many websites trying to find one that would look just right. Dark green with a slinky neckline and cut to the knee. Dressy but not over the top.

I fussed with my makeup for more than an hour, trying to get it just right before slipping on the dress, smoothing it down with my palms.

Neil smiled as I opened the door, casting his eyes over me. "You look amazing."

My heart stopped. Did he mean it in a fatherly way, or was it more an 'I'd hump you into next week' kind of comment? "Thanks."

"Ready to show off your work?"

I grinned. "This is the bit that makes me nervous. Not that it really matters. Renee will claim all of the credit."

He held out his arm for me to link mine through. "What

matters is that we both know the truth. That you're the one with all the talent."

I slid my arm in his. "I'm glad you know that. Of all the customers."

"One day, you will be the shining light. Don't you worry about that. Renee Jameson will have to work out how to keep her head above water once she loses the woman who really runs the show."

This was so confusing. He was so close, and I could smell his lightly scented aftershave. I couldn't possibly feel this way, but some part of me knew I was falling in love.

"Let's get going."

I nodded my assent and we walked toward the door. He opened it and I walked through first, with him right after me. All the way to the elevator, I felt his eyes on me, and I held my breath, hoping he was taking in how I looked from behind. I'd always been told I had a nice arse.

If he had, he showed no sign of it as we entered the lift, laughing as we both reached for the ground floor button at the same time. Our hands touched, and this time the spark between us was undeniable as we withdrew and stared at one another.

His eyes were so confused, and I understood more than he would ever know. How could feeling this way be right?

Looking into his eyes, I saw so much of what my heart had been telling me. There was so much more to this than just friendship, or him offering work to his daughter's friend, or even the attraction he'd admitted to feeling.

He swallowed, smiling as the look disappeared from his

eyes, his confidence returning. The lift bell went and the doors opened, neither of us moving for a moment.

"Shall we get out of the lift?" he said, raising his eyebrows.

No, I want you to throw me against the wall and have your way with me.

"Sure."

I trailed behind him through the lift exit and toward the car parked outside. I didn't touch him, link my arm with him —that would be way too awkward after our moment. He opened the passenger door, waving me in with a smile as I sank into that beautiful leather seat.

When he climbed into the driver's side, I gave him a lazy smile. "I love your car."

"I know."

"You might have to wake me up when we get to your offices." I couldn't help making that joke one last time.

He laughed, shaking his head. "It's not *that* far."

Still, I might have closed my eyes for a while as the car purred down the road.

After a quiet ten-minute drive we pulled into the car park. There wasn't an empty space in sight, and I smiled as we drove straight into Neil's personal spot. At least we wouldn't have to drive around looking.

Neil stopped. "I'll get the door."

My heart fluttered as he walked around, opening my door and smiling as I climbed out.

This wasn't good.

Renee stood at the front door of the building with Neil's

PA, welcoming guests. She fixed her eyes on me, looking me up and down with such a sour expression. Then she saw Neil.

"Oh. Neil. I had no idea you were bringing Nicola with you." She smiled that fake smile she gave all the customers.

"I have to admit I was surprised she wasn't on the original guest list. I decided to take matters into my own hands." He reached for my hand, squeezing it and smiling at me. I shook like a leaf.

Renee stiffened. "You look lovely, Nicola. The green goes so well with your eyes."

Right now it's kind of the same colour as you.

"Thank you."

She gave us another one of those smiles, and we walked past her and into the crowd of Neil's customers. At least here I could forget everything for a while. As long as we steered clear of my boss, the evening should be good.

Everyone else was so lovely and Neil guided me through the room, never leaving me alone for a second.

"It's time to make my speech. Come on."

I trailed behind him, stopping at the front as the crowd gathered around, his PA moving through the stragglers to bring them over.

Neil cleared his throat. "I'd like to thank Renee Jameson and Jameson Interiors for the amazing job they've done with the place. They've dragged me into the 21st century. Most of all, I'd like to thank Nicola Crandell for coming up with a design that an old guy like me could appreciate, as well as the younger members of staff."

I gaped, having not realised that he was going to mention my name at all. There would be hell to pay on Monday for that. Renee would take her anger out on me.

The rest of his speech was a blur, but my skin tingled as I felt so many eyes my way. I turned my head, locking gazes with Renee, the irritation in her eyes clear as she narrowed them at me. I hadn't asked Neil to say anything; I hadn't thought he would. She would think I was behind it. If I knew her at all, she'd already taken all of the credit among his customers.

After his speech, he took a step and headed straight for me as the crowd broke up, so much pride in his eyes, I wanted to cry.

"Thank you," I said as he approached.

"Did you really think I wasn't going to tell the world who really did the work?"

I licked my lips, swallowing to give myself courage to say the next thing that I had to. "This is going to make things really awkward for me. I'm already getting evil looks."

His face fell, the disappointment clear.

My heart broke a little to see it. The last thing I wanted to do was upset him when he was so proud of me. "I am grateful. It's nice to feel appreciated."

"More than appreciated." *What the hell did that mean?* He smiled, the warmth back in his eyes. "How about a wine?"

"That would be lovely."

"I'll go and track down a couple of glasses. We'll have a toast to your success."

I nodded, watching as he walked away. My stomach ached at the thought of upsetting him. All he wanted to do was to tell the world who had done the work. I'd never had a client do anything like this before, but then again, they usually didn't know I was the designer.

"What was that all about?" Renee pounced as soon as he was gone.

"I don't know. He didn't tell me he was going to do that."

"What are you even here for? You know that *I* attend these launches."

I glared at her. "He invited me. What was I supposed to do? Say 'Sorry, but Renee forbids me to go'? It's his launch and he's a friend of *my* family."

I'd never stood up to her like this, and it was obvious she had no idea how to deal with it as she backed away. "We'll talk about this on Monday."

"I'm sure we will."

Her darkness disappeared as the shining light that was Neil reappeared with two glasses of champagne. "Renee."

"Neil. I was just saying to Nicola what a lovely speech that was. It's not often a client recognises the huge amount of work we *all* do to provide our service." She smiled sweetly.

"Of course. I'm sure everyone worked very hard," he said. I flicked a glance between them. Two strong people, neither of whom had any inclination to back down.

To break the deadlock, I reached for my champagne, prompting a warm smile from Neil. "Nicola. There are some more people I'd like you to meet." He nodded. "Renee."

I caught my breath at the weight of his hand in the small of my back, smiling at Renee as I moved on with Neil right behind me.

It had been a long time since I'd felt so alive.

This night could go on forever.

I SHIVERED as we left the building, every hair on my body standing to attention in the cool breeze. At least it wasn't far to the car.

"How much do you weigh?" Neil's blue eyes pierced my own before he frowned. "Sorry, that was rude and none of my business. There's nothing of you, and you must be freezing."

I shrugged. "We'll be inside soon."

"And I'll be nursing you with pneumonia. Here." He pulled off his jacket, draping it over my shoulders. The warm, soft wool enveloped me, and I pulled it tight around me. It smelled of him, and I smiled a little.

"Better?"

"Now you're cold."

"At least you're not freezing to death." He smiled, and the heat in my cheeks rose as his gaze stayed on me. I wasn't used to being under quite so much scrutiny. At least not from someone I was this attracted to.

His hand on my back again made me sigh as he guided me to the car. As independent as I was, I liked his attentiveness, his caring, his putting me first as he opened the door for me. Whatever happened after this evening, this had been the most amazing night of my life, and it wasn't even a date.

Neil climbed into the driver's seat and smiled. "Let's get you home."

I don't want to go home. I want to stay right here with you.

I forced my lips into a nervous smile, and he narrowed his eyes as he took it in. "Are you okay?"

Nodding, I pushed that smile up a little more. How could I tell him I was simply overwhelmed by his kindness, the acts seeming to be second nature to him? Why couldn't I have ever found a man like him?

He turned the key, and the engine purred as I leaned back in my seat.

We drove through the streets in silence, but it was comfortable, and I snuggled down into the leather seat, drowning in the luxuriousness of the Audi and the softness of his jacket.

"Don't fall asleep." His voice broke the quiet, and I flicked a glance at him. He looked back at me, my heart fluttering from the intimate smile on his face.

We pulled up outside my apartment block, and he was out of the car and around to open my door in a flash.

"I'll walk you in," he said.

This was it. After tonight, there were no more reasons for us to spend time together. I'd enjoy the last few minutes of his company and then work out how to fill the void his absence would create in my life.

When we reached the door, I fumbled in my clutch purse to find the key, and slid it slowly into the lock.

"I suppose I'd better give you your jacket back." I slid it off my shoulders, and turned back toward him. He gripped it, and I lingered as I let go.

"Good night, Nicola. Sleep well." He bent to kiss me, catching the edge of my mouth.

We gazed at one another for just a moment, his eyebrows

knitting together as he frowned, clearly concerned about my reaction.

I said nothing, my heart pounding so hard, not wanting to pull away.

He reached up, stroking my hair and searching my face. Maybe he thought I'd move back, but right at this moment I was where I wanted to be.

I swallowed hard. "Want to come in for coffee?"

Reaching for the door handle behind me, I pushed, slowly walking backward into the apartment. For every step I took, he moved with me, pushing the door shut.

"I don't want coffee," he said, just so matter-of-factly. My heart beat even faster if that were at all possible and I stopped.

Neil moved forward until he stood toe to toe with me, our bodies only inches apart.

"Neither do I." The words came out before I could stop them, and in an instant his lips were on mine, pressing gently, lingering before he growled, kissing me harder. He wrapped his arms around my waist, pulling me to him.

I'd never been kissed like this before.

The warmth of his hands disappeared as he pulled back, his eyes full of confusion. This was a man so sure of himself, so confident, but right now he just looked scared.

"I can't do this," he said.

I nodded, my eyesight bleary from the teardrops that ran down my cheeks.

"Go home," I whispered.

"Nicola, I ..." He shrugged helplessly, swallowing hard as he kept his gaze fixed on my face.

"Just go, *Mr Wallace.*"

He frowned, but stayed in the same spot, not moving, just looking at me. "I'm sorry," he said quietly.

"You have nothing to be sorry for."

"It's just that ..." He exhaled, the strain on his face obvious. He was as torn as I was about all of this. "When I'm near you, I want what I don't think I can have."

I licked my lips, slowing my breathing deliberately. "I want what you want. I think."

"How, Nicola?"

Now I moved forward, placing my hands on the collar of his shirt, gripping the lapels tight so as to not let him get away. "Stay with me."

I shook as I said the words, terrified that he would take up the offer, but at the same time wanting him so much that nothing else mattered—not my boss, not his daughter. If he wanted me, nothing would keep me from him.

For one long moment we looked, just looked. Tension strung taut between us.

In an instant his mouth was on mine, kissing me hard as I pulled him toward me. I wanted everything—the kiss, his touch, this man inside me. I'd never needed anything so much in my whole life. It didn't matter to me if it was just for tonight. He was mine.

I closed my eyes as he pulled away, too scared to open them in case he was gone and I was all alone.

"Nicola," he said, so soft and tender. My insides melted at his tone.

Swallowing hard, I licked my lips again, trembling as I gazed into his eyes. Every little emotion was on display from a man who usually covered his feelings with a professional front.

"Are you going to stay?" I whispered.

He scrutinised me, reaching up and gripping my hair. "Is that what you really want?"

"I want you."

EIGHT

HE TRAILED behind me into my bedroom, his hands on my back. I came to a stop at the end of the bed, turning toward him.

Raising his hands to cup my face, he gazed into my eyes, a smile creeping across his lips.

"What?"

"Let me look at you," he whispered, brushing his lips over mine.

He was intoxicating. His firm grip on my face left me unable to pull away. Not that I wanted to.

"Don't tease me."

Neil shook his head. "I'm not planning to. I want this as much as you do."

He kissed me again, and in his arms with his lips on mine, tasting his tongue as he deepened the kiss, I forgot about the outside world. For now, it was us, just us, and nothing else would intrude on this moment.

His hands were at my neck, brushing my skin as he pulled the zip down the back of my dress. This was it. I could freak out about how wrong this was, or I could let myself go and just enjoy the moment.

I let go.

Pressing my hands to his chest, I unhooked his shirt buttons one by one.

"I've been wanting to do this since that first day I saw you again." He pressed kisses by my ear, down my neck, leaving me gasping as I pulled my arms out of the sleeves of my dress, letting it fall to the floor. I pushed back his shirt. He was in good shape, and clearly took care of himself.

"Get onto the bed." His tone sent shivers up my spine. This was a man used to getting his own way, and I wasn't about to object.

Dropping his pants to the floor, he climbed onto the bed beside me, running his gaze up and down my body.

"You're so beautiful," he whispered, and I teared up just looking at him. I'd had boyfriends say that to me before, but not in the tone he'd used. It would be so easy to fall in love with this gentle, kind man whose control oozed out of him.

"Thank you." The words were all I could manage.

He laughed, reaching over and rolling me slightly, unhooking my bra as he grinned. "You are blushing like crazy."

"I don't mean to."

"Want to stop?" He took a deep breath, as if he was afraid of the answer.

I shook my head. "I've been thinking about this for weeks."

"So have I." His eyes danced away, avoiding direct contact. He acted like a nervous teenager.

I gulped. "So ..."

"So ..." He pulled my bra down my arms, and I shook as my breasts were revealed. They'd never been big, but I was proud of how perky they were.

A smile spread across his lips as he reached one hand up, cupping a breast and running this thumb across my nipple. It pebbled at his touch, and I caught my breath.

He lowered his head, taking my nipple in his mouth and sucking gently. I ran my fingers through his hair, sighing at this new intimacy between us. There was no going back now.

"Is this really what you want, Nicola?" he asked.

"There's nothing I want more."

At that his mouth devoured mine, his kisses growing with intensity as he pulled me close. This was it. This man who I really shouldn't be with was about to become my lover. Whether it be for one night or more, my life would never be the same.

My mind went blank as he ran his fingers down my leg, slipping them inside my panties and finding that spot that left my eyes rolling back in my head and a smile spreading on my face before I knew it.

"I like that reaction," Neil murmured, and I refocused, fixing my gaze on his.

I laughed, clearing my throat. "That was so hot."

"I like that reaction even more." He laughed, scanning my features. "I love your voice. So sexy."

My raspy voice had often made me stand out from the crowd. Not always in a good way. I hated it. As he spoke, his fingers pushed at me more insistently, and I thrust my hips back and forward to rub myself against him. This damn man would have me crying his name as I came, and neither of us were fully naked yet.

"Is there anything in particular you like?" he asked, bending his head and scraping his teeth across my nipple. If he didn't do something more soon, I'd have to roll over and do it for him. Maybe that was what he wanted.

"I like this," I answered a little quickly, his devilish laugh telling me he knew exactly how much I liked it.

"Sometimes I like to take things fast, sometimes slow. I want you so badly, but at the same time I want to savour the moment of our first time together."

First time together. That must mean he isn't going to screw me and run.

"I know what you mean." My cheeks blazed hot as his fingers kept rubbing. I wanted him so much, but I wanted this feeling to last forever.

"I like being in charge."

There it was, out in the open. I'd suspected as much, but what did that entail? "In what way?"

He kissed my breasts gently before seeking out my lips. His mouth was warm, and the taste of his kiss left me limp in his arms. I loved every little thing about him. "Nothing bad. I just like doing things my way. If you want to complain, I could always tie you to the bed."

I gaped at him, and a sneaky smile spread across his lips. No matter how horrified I might look, the truth was I wanted him inside me more than anything.

"Maybe I'd complain on purpose," I whispered.

With a growl he pulled away from me, pulling down my panties and sending them flying off the end of the bed.

I giggled as he rolled on top of me, kissing me with so much force I was sure my lips would bruise. One thing was clear. He wanted me. A lot.

Trailing kisses down between my breasts and over my stomach, he buried himself between my legs, his tongue leaving me gasping and groaning. *Rebecca's father is going down on me.*

Okay. That was weird. I threw that thought out of my head. He was Neil, the man I'd spent weeks getting to know, the man I wanted as much as he wanted me.

And holy cow, was he showing how much he wanted me. I reached down to run my fingers through his hair. He growled again, grabbing my hands with his own and linking our fingers in such an intimate gesture, I sighed.

A warm feeling grew in my stomach, spreading up my body, and I moaned as I hit my climax, pushing against him. He groaned, and I squeezed his hands still linked in mine to show how much I enjoyed his attentions.

Neil raised his head, a satisfied grin on his face. "Happy?"

"Very."

For a moment, I thought he might remove his pants and join me. Instead, he buried his face again until I shook and shuddered, crying out his name as the heat overtook me.

Now he knelt, pulling his wallet out of his pants pocket. From it, he produced a condom packet. "Last chance to back out."

"Hurry up." I grinned, grabbing both sides of my pillow and pulling myself up. I needed him inside me.

As he rolled the condom on, I licked my lips at the size of him. That was unexpected.

"You okay?" Neil asked. I blinked, raising my gaze to his face. His brows were furrowed in concern.

"I'm fine."

He smiled, leaning over my body and kissing me softly as he pushed into me. I was filled by this beautiful, gentle man, who began to move inside me, his kisses moving from my lips to my neck to my shoulder before he took one of my nipples into his mouth.

Overwhelmed by this feeling of being wanted, all I could do was run my hands down his back as he thrust, feeling his smooth skin. I raised my foot and brought my knee up, giving him more room to move, and he mumbled his appreciation as he switched to the other breast.

Every touch drove me crazy, his hands and mouth on my body stirring some dormant feeling that I'd thought long since buried. I'd had fast sex and slow sex, but never felt so whole, so perfectly matched with another human being.

He ran his hand up my side, linking fingers with mine again. This wasn't just sex for him, either—not the way he was acting. The connection we shared was much deeper than that. It was big and scary, but I wouldn't be anywhere else right now.

"Nicola," he whispered. His eyes were so full of wonder.

"It's been a very long time since I felt this connected with anyone."

My chest ached as if it were about to burst at his words. I was unique—this wasn't his usual routine. I could have wept at the joy in my heart, the newfound knowledge filling me with the desire to keep him here in my bed, in my life.

He groaned as he came, stilling over me as he kissed me deeply. I didn't want him to pull out, and I don't think he wanted to either. He lingered before sighing and rolling onto his back.

"I'll just get rid of this. Where's the bathroom?" he asked as he stripped off the condom.

"Out the door and just to the left." I watched as he rolled out of bed and walked out the door. He was just as nice to look at from behind as he was from the front, and I sighed at just how perfectly the evening had turned out.

Still in my dream-like state, I jumped when the bed sunk, Neil climbing back in beside me.

"Come here. Let's see if we can get some sleep after that."

"I think I could sleep for a week." I snuggled into his arms and stroked his smooth chest, smiling smugly at the knowledge he was mine, at least tonight. For the first time in a long time, I was truly happy.

"Tell me what you're thinking about."

"How happy I am. I wanted this so badly—I never thought you'd want it too."

He rubbed my arm. "I'd have to be crazy not to want that."

I chewed my lip and sighed. "I'm also one of the last people you should be involved with."

Neil brought his hand around, tilting my chin to meet his gaze. "This isn't going to be easy. Not if we both want to keep seeing one another."

"Is that what you want?"

He placed his palm on my cheek, his blue eyes smiling. "I would never have stayed if I didn't want more."

I exhaled loudly. "Phew. I thought you might just want this to be a one-off."

"And you still let me into your bed?"

I nuzzled his hand. "I just wanted you."

"I noticed how much you enjoyed it." He grinned and kissed me, his lips soft and warm against mine, and despite the ache between my legs, I was happy to go again if he was up for it.

"I loved it. No one's ever cared so much about making me feel good."

His brows knitted together and he cocked his head, frowning at me. "I thought of nothing else but how good I wanted to make you feel. You're perfect."

I smiled, dropping my gaze, and shook my head. "I'm far from perfect."

"Maybe that's what you think, but I can tell you now it's not true. You're a beautiful, intelligent, talented woman. I think you hide behind the makeup and the clothing, but you're incredible."

No one had ever said anything like that to me before, and I teared up before I could fight it. No one had ever truly appreciated the real me, except for my parents.

"Did you ever think about settling down again?" I asked, needing to change the subject from me to him.

"Rebecca was my focus. Her mother let her down so many times. I didn't think I could do that to anyone else. So, I had a vasectomy. It just made things less complicated."

I looked back into his eyes. "That was a bit extreme. You still used a condom tonight."

He shrugged. "I'm clean. I have regular physical exams, but I never want to risk hurting anyone. It's just safer."

"You're a good man."

"Am I?"

"I think so." I pecked his lips.

"One thing I do remember is you ending up in hospital at some stage. Rebecca worried so much about how little you ate."

I sighed. "It got a little ridiculous at one point, and I will admit I struggle sometimes, but I'm a long way from where I was back then. Finding out I probably wouldn't have children helped me work that out."

His expression was pained. "Nicola."

Shrugging, I ran my fingers down his arm again. "It's not like I could do much about it now. At one stage in my life it was what I wanted—now I know there's a good chance it'll never happen, it's not so bad."

"I had no idea."

"The only people who knew were my parents and the boyfriend I was trying to have a baby with at the time. In the past." I propped myself up on my elbow and kissed his shoulder.

Neil raised his hand to my head, gazing at me. "I like this." He stroked my hair, running his eyes over my face.

"So do I." I nestled into his chest, planting a kiss on it before closing my eyes. I'd sleep like a baby after the most amazing sex I'd ever had. Even if he changed his mind, I had tonight.

Tonight was all I needed.

HE DIDN'T RUN.

He didn't freak out and leave in the night. When I woke, the warmth of his body still radiated in my bed, and I propped myself up on the pillow with my elbow to watch him.

Neil mumbled something in his sleep, nothing that made any sense, and I couldn't help myself. I pressed my lips to his forehead, wanting to be close to him before he woke.

His eyes flickered open at the touch, and he smiled at me with that warm, sexy smile that undid me the night before.

"Good morning," he said.

I couldn't find any words, laughing before I realised what I was doing, my heart beating so fast I thought it might escape my chest. He gave me crazy butterflies.

"Nicola. Are you okay?" One eyebrow quirked, and I swore I could see him thinking the same thing. Worried I'd freak about about what we'd done.

"Better than okay." I spoke the words, my lips refusing to crack the grin that swept them. This was permanent when I was with him.

"I'm glad." He reached up, stroking my hair, his gaze sweeping over my face. "I was worried you'd have regrets this morning."

"Never," I whispered.

He leaned forward just a little, brushing my lips with his.

"If you're worried about me having any, don't be. I can't help myself when I'm with you."

He kissed me again, this time more forcefully, and I surrendered to it, not wanting him to stop. The kiss deepened as his grip in my hair tightened, and I rubbed my body against his, feeling him harden, knowing it was me he wanted.

"Damn it, Nicola."

"Yes?" I tried to sweeten my voice, make myself sound innocent.

"It isn't supposed to feel this good." He nuzzled my ear, burying himself in my neck as his hand stroked my breasts. His hands were so warm and strong, and I closed my eyes, relaxing at his touch.

As he trailed kisses down between my breasts and over my stomach, I wriggled when he reached the top of my thighs.

"Stay still." His voice was serious, commanding. It sent a shiver up my spine, but I was in no mood for that.

"No." I reached down, running my fingers through his hair.

He grabbed my wrists, pinning them to my sides, caressing my arms with his thumbs.

"If you can't stay still, I'll hold you there."

Damn it. He must have been a gym bunny like his daughter. His grip was as strong as his tone—I couldn't move my hands to touch him.

Neil bent his head, tonguing my clit as I bucked my hips, trying to get away but wanting more and more. And he gave me more, moaning as he sucked gently, claiming that hot spot between my legs for his own. I don't know where he learned his oral skills, but he could do this to me as long and as often as he wanted.

"Neil," I cried out as my orgasm overtook me. The urge to pull my hands away overwhelmed me, but I couldn't move, held to the bed by his firm grip.

He was relentless. Each time I came, he went straight back to it, licking and sucking, possessing. Not being able to touch him or move just made me come harder. There was no getting away from him—not that I was really trying.

He continued his assault, and I rode his tongue, moving the only part of my body I could, grinding against his face. It was deliciously dirty and hot all in one.

His hands let go of my wrists, and he squeezed my thighs as he brought me to orgasm one more time. Panting, I grabbed his biceps as he climbed over me, kissing me deeply, rubbing his naked body to mine.

"What you do to me, Nicola," he said, almost sounding mournful.

"What do I do to you?" I asked, already knowing the answer. He was hard against my leg and I rocked my hips, pushing closer to my target.

"I've never wanted anyone so much. To touch you, to taste you."

"I want you inside me," I whispered.

"I want to be inside you, but I have no more condoms. Do you?"

He pushed two fingers inside me and I moaned, thrusting and riding them. I could do this for hours. He made me feel so good.

"No, but we don't need a condom if you've had a vasectomy."

The fingers stopped and he studied my face, his eyebrows knitting together in confusion. I shrugged. The moment was ruined anyway—why not keep on ruining it?

"I'm clean. I'm sure you are. You didn't want to touch Renee, after all." I poked my tongue out, and he roared with laughter.

"You are being a very wicked young woman, suggesting nasty things about your boss."

I waggled my eyebrows. "Come and get me if you want to see nasty."

Neil grinned. "Why, Miss Crandell, a man could think you were trying to corrupt him."

I laughed. It sounded even throatier than usual first thing in the morning. "Oh, I think it's far too late for that."

He kissed me, and we were both gone, lost in one another as we drifted further and further from going back to the way things used to be.

Nothing would ever be the same.

AFTER A WEEKEND mostly spent in bed, I could barely walk on Monday morning, but I smiled at the ache and hugged myself at the memory of Neil's touch. As exhausted as I was, I didn't want it to stop and I sat at my desk, subdued, tired, happy.

"Have you got the plan ready for the Duncan refit?"

I'd been sitting down for five minutes when Renee pounced, and it took everything in me to stop rolling my eyes.

"I do. I finished it last night." After Neil had gone home, I'd spent the rest of the evening drawing like crazy, inspired by my happy heart.

She smiled that snarky smile, and I knew something bitchy was about to come out of her mouth. "Good to see you've got something done on time." She turned, the bangles on her wrist jingling as she reached for her office door handle.

"Oh, by the way." The snarky smile now resembled that of a shark. Whatever was coming was bound to be a slap in the face. I braced myself. "I'll be attending a function tonight with Neil Wallace. Thank you *so* much for introducing me to him."

I stared after her as she swanned into her office and disappeared, the door slamming behind her. He was going out with her? After ... after everything we'd done together? After I'd given myself to him with such abandon? After I'd cried his name again and again as he played my body like a musician strokes an instrument?

My stomach sunk to my knees as I opened the file on the computer and pressed send. My joy had turned dark. Had he used me? He'd known me for half my life, and what was I to him? Some silly little play-thing that clearly meant nothing.

What you do to me, Nicola.

His words still echoed in my head, as if I was someone special to him. Someone he had feelings for.

I blinked back the tears as Tamara came in and took her seat. "Hey, Nicola. Have a good weekend?"

"It was wonderful," I said.

"Yeah?"

"I ..."

"Oooh someone's got an admirer." Cherie's voice came from behind me, and I turned around to see her standing in the doorway with an enormous bundle of roses. Red and white roses, to be precise.

Now I let the eye roll go. Was this for Renee? I'd climbed so high and sunk so low already this morning, they couldn't possibly be for me.

Cherie waltzed up to my desk, laying them gently on the surface while I stared.

"What have *you* been up to, Miss Nicola?" She looked down at me, her eyebrows raised as if waiting for an answer.

"I am *so* googling what red and white roses mean." Tamara laughed.

I let myself smile just a little, plucking the card from the envelope on the side of the bouquet.

Hoping this brightens your day. Neil.

My heart pounded at a billion beats per minute as I read the words over and over again. But he had a date with Renee. What the hell was going on?

"So, red means love or passion. White means innocence or purity. Together they mean unity," Tamara said.

Was he sending me a message, or were they just colours that he liked? This whole thing was doing my head in. Being with Neil was either the most incredible thing I'd ever done, or the most stupid.

Renee's door opened with a click. "Nicola, can you please email me the ..." I looked up at her. One of her eyebrows arched a lot more than the other. It was usually so hard to tell —she had them groomed in an over-the-top fashion to begin with.

"Nicola?"

I smiled.

"Oh, but they're lovely. Who are they from?"

I was serene. She couldn't hurt me, not with these beautiful flowers on my desk. Even if I didn't know Neil's reasoning for sending them.

Somewhere in the distance, the phone rang.

"A friend."

"A friend sends you red roses? Congratulations."

Cherie coughed. "Nicola, there's a call for you."

Renee leaned over, taking a deep breath and smiling. "Maybe if I'm a good girl tonight, someone special will send me roses."

My skin burned with indignation. Like hell Neil would ever feel for her her in that way. Even if he didn't want more from me than just the other night, I would make sure he never ended up with her.

"Anyway, I'll let you take your call. Please email me with the costings for the Duncan refit. It's not in the email you forwarded."

I nodded, seething as she turned away and disappeared into the office.

"Cherie, can you put it through?" It was probably Katya with some invite to something. Since she got engaged, she kept asking me for colour advice for bridesmaids' dresses and other assorted things. She'd outshine everyone else at the wedding, but I'd told her to just dress them in beige.

I picked up the phone. "Nicola Crandell."

The last voice I expected to hear was the deep one that greeted me. "Nicola."

I froze, Neil's voice sending tingles down my spine, remembering his touch, remembering his words. *What you do to me, Nicola.* I could still feel his hands holding my wrists down, stopping me from touching him as he pleasured me with his tongue. The thought of that alone made me want to escape somewhere private.

"Hi," I squeaked. Tamara's head shot up, her lips curling into a sly smile.

"I wanted to make sure the flowers arrived. I'm sorry for

calling you at work; I tried your mobile first, but it went to voicemail." He sounded warm, caring.

"They did. Thank you so much."

"It was the least I could do. After our time together."

What did that mean? That our time together was over?

"They're beautiful," I managed to get out.

"Beautiful flowers for a beautiful woman. What are you doing tonight?"

Tonight? *Oh, I don't know. Sitting around pining after having the most amazing sex ever while you go out with my boss?*

"Nothing much. Probably curl up on the couch with a cup of hot chocolate and watch TV."

"Want some company?"

My heart fluttered, and I must have been smiling like an idiot as I waved at Tamara to sit as she bounced up and down in her seat.

"If you don't have anything else to do."

He sighed. "I do have a prior commitment. It's the Chamber of Commerce dinner tonight, and I'm giving a presentation beforehand about business finance. But I will get out as early as I can to come and see you. If you want me to."

I didn't want anything else—wouldn't be able to *think* about anything else. I'd tackle the Renee question when I saw him. "Yes."

"You do? I was so scared that after the weekend, that would be it. I can get a little intense."

I turned my chair so the back was facing Tamara. "Maybe I like intense," I whispered.

"Maybe I could text you what I like. Maybe you can text

me back with what you like." He had lowered his voice, as if this was an adventure. A big, dirty adventure.

"My phone has no money on it at the moment. It'd be a one-sided conversation." I laughed.

"Oh. Scratch that idea, then. I'll have to tell you tonight. If I can keep my hands off you long enough to have a conversation."

Holy ...

"So, what time will you be at my place? So we can have this talk?"

He laughed. "Are you trying to distract me from talking dirty now? Because that is where this is headed."

"I'm at work. Not appropriate," I said, laughing.

"Who said anything about appropriate? I was hoping to get inappropriate later."

"Later."

"I'll come by tonight, maybe around eight-thirty?"

I closed my eyes. "I'll look forward to it."

TFN

I DIDN'T EVEN KNOW what was on television. All I did know was that the hands on the wall clock moved too slow for my liking. All I could think about was Neil.

My beautiful flowers were in a vase on the coffee table. They looked huge on the small wooden surface, but I wanted them in sight. Near me.

I alternated between looking at the clock and looking at the flowers. There were a million questions I wanted to ask Neil—what he wanted from me, where this was going ... But then again, we'd been flirting for what felt like forever before we'd slept together; this wasn't just a flash in the pan.

Although we hadn't exactly done a lot of sleeping.

Lost in thought, I jumped when the phone rang. Reaching for it, I picked it up, rolling my eyes at the number.

"Hey, Katya."

"You were right. Beige."

I smiled to my myself, trying hard not to laugh out loud.

"I told you. Let them fade away into the background while you take up all of the glory."

"Yes." She sounded so pleased with herself. "What are you up to? Want to go out for a drink?"

"Thanks for the offer, but I'm having a quiet night in. Work was just diabolical today."

"Oh, see you at our next lunch, then. I just wanted to say thank you for a wonderful idea."

"No problem. Let me know if you need any more help."

Tap-tap-tap.

Shit.

"Sure thing. Have a nice night."

I hung up, throwing the phone on the table as I ran to the door. There could only be one person standing on the other side, and no sooner had I flung the door open than Neil had me in his arms, attempting to kiss my lips off.

I walked backward as he pushed forward, kicking the door shut behind him, and we stood at the entrance to my flat, making out like a pair of teenagers who couldn't keep their hands off one another. I wanted him to take me, consume me.

His lips grazed my neck as he pulled me closer. "I got out of there as soon as I could."

I grabbed his wrist, pulling him to the bedroom, unbuttoning my shirt with my free hand as I went and flinging it to the floor as we made it in the door.

"Nicola," he moaned as I reached for his pants, having him unbuttoned and unzipped in an instant. My mind was full of him, wanting him, needing him. I pushed down his underwear. He stood at the foot of my bed with an erection that any man would envy.

"I've been thinking about this all day." I dropped to my knees, taking charge and pulling him into my mouth, running my tongue from the tip of his cock all the way down, tasting him.

"I've thought about nothing else but you." He ran his fingers through my hair, not pushing me like other boyfriends had done in the past, but touching me gently. Caring, but in control.

As I sped up, he groaned, spurring me on as I claimed this man. No one else would ever make him feel this good. Not Renee—no one but me. At the thought of her getting this close to him, tears rolled down my cheeks. What a sight I must look. Neil had put me first the other night, and here I was, giving the blow job of my life and I was crying.

"Nicola?" He'd noticed, lifting me gently until I stood, looking at me with a mixture of hurt and confusion. "What's wrong?"

"I'm sorry. Just stupid thoughts and now I've ruined the moment."

"What thoughts?"

He wrapped his arms around my shoulders, pulling me in tight. His erection pressed against my belly, a constant reminder of how much he wanted me.

"This is so stupid." I pulled back, kneeling again, but before I could take him in my mouth, he dropped to the floor.

"You could never be stupid. Tell me what's wrong."

"Were you out with Renee tonight?"

His eyebrows shot straight up. "Why would you think that? I told you, it was the Chamber of Commerce annual dinner. She was there, but I didn't speak with her."

"She made it sound like you were on a date."

He scowled, pulling me to him again and I collapsed against his body, a shivering, miserable mess.

"Why on earth would you think I'd be on a date with her when all I can think about is you?"

"I don't know why."

Neil slipped his fingers under my chin and raising my eyes to meet his.

"I know I shouldn't, but all I want is to bury myself in you and never emerge. There is nothing more on this planet I want than to lose myself in you," he whispered.

He stroked my cheeks with his thumbs, wiping away my tears. "Nicola, I don't know where this is going, and I don't know what you want, but the only woman I want to be with right now is you."

Bending his head, he brushed my lips with his in a reassuring kiss that left me breathless. He stood, pulling me to my feet and guiding me to the bed where he pulled back the blanket, undressing me, running his hands down my body as he pushed me to sit.

He walked around the bed as I pulled the blanket over me, dropping his clothes to the floor before climbing in beside me. In his arms, I felt safe, content.

"Tell me what Renee said to upset you."

I pouted. "Do I have to?"

"We were having one hell of a sexy moment there, and

something made you sad. I want to know what it is." There it was, that in-control tone. Did he ever have any angry moments where he just spun out and lost it? He said all the right words when it came to making me feel, but what was behind it? I'd been so intimate with him and yet I didn't really know him at all.

"She said she was attending a function with you tonight. She thanked me for introducing you."

He pulled me tighter to him. "Did you really think I was going out with her?"

I raised my eyes to meet his, and found concern. He cared so much about my answer, more than I'd expected. I'd been so scared that he would run for the hills after our night together, but he was here with me, making sure I was okay.

"I didn't know," I said in a tiny voice. I'd never had anyone to hold me when I was upset and insecure. I'd had boyfriends, but only a couple of serious ones.

Part of my problem was that I'd always been so preoccupied about creating the perfect impression. I might do it all myself, but my grooming was immaculate, and I'd tried to stay as skinny as I thought the men in my life liked. Sometimes, I hated myself for it, and would gorge with food and then live with regret.

I didn't have a healthy relationship with myself. How could I have one with anyone else?

"I'm not interested in dating Renee Jameson, or any other woman. For weeks, you and only you have been under my skin, and now I've given in to the constant temptation I'm not letting you go. All I can do is to hope you feel the same way, and judging from this, I think you do."

I nodded. This whole thing overwhelmed me, and I knew I'd have to let him see that without scaring him off. It didn't look like he was easily scared.

"We've got a lot to work through. I don't want to tell anyone about us just yet because I want us to have a chance to see where this goes. But, sweetheart, it's been a long time since any woman made me feel the way you do, and I wouldn't risk that for anything."

"I'm scared," I croaked the words as he stroked my arm, my skin tingling at his touch. He had a way of making me feel safe and yet on edge.

Neil smiled. "As am I. This is new territory for me, too. I don't want to hurt Rebecca, but I can't keep away from you. In time I'll tell her, but right now I want you all to myself."

He leaned over, burying his face in my neck, planting gentle kisses on my collarbone, leaving me gasping as his hand trailed down my body, slowing at my breast and burrowing between my legs.

"We can be scared together," he whispered, his fingers finding my clit. He gently rubbed while he kissed me, long and deep, and I was lost, not wanting to be anywhere else but in his arms.

THE INCESSANT CHIME of the alarm clock made me groan as I felt for the snooze button. We'd curled up to sleep at a reasonably decent hour. It had been a Monday night after all, and we both had work in the morning.

I turned my head to the right, smiling at the man with a grin on his face, who nuzzled my cheek and kissed me.

"I like waking up with you," he whispered.

"I like waking up with you, even if it is stupid o'clock and I must look like crap."

Neil laughed. "You're always beautiful."

I was never any good at taking compliments. I looked away, my cheeks getting hot at his words.

He reached for my chin, pulling me back to look at him. "You don't think a lot of yourself at times, do you?"

I shrugged. "I don't know. I'm not smart like Rebecca, or calculating like Katya. Or Gemma, the trust-fund baby who is so gorgeous she models sometimes."

Neil sighed, kissing me softly. "You don't give yourself enough credit. Not only are you a beautiful woman, you're incredibly smart. You're so talented, Nicola. You should start your own design company. Give Renee Jameson the flick."

With what? I couldn't support myself while I started up a business of my own. Mum and Dad weren't in a position to help me out. But I wasn't about to say that to Neil. I'd seen his house, knew his business was worth a lot of money. Rebecca was really down to earth, but she'd never wanted for anything. We lived in the same world, but were from different ones.

"It's not that simple."

"I could help you."

I recoiled from his touch. That was the last thing I wanted.

"Nicola?"

"I can't take money from you, if that's what you're talking about."

He frowned, keeping eye contact. It was unnerving to say the least. The expression on his face was one of disappointment, but with a big dose of confusion. "What if I want to help you?"

"I don't want someone to pay my way for me. I have to work my life out for myself."

Neil smiled. "I bought Rebecca a business to get her started; I just thought we could do something for you."

"I'm not your daughter." I snapped before I could help it, and he moved away, his eyes so full of hurt. He hadn't meant to upset me, but I could just picture what people would think. That I only wanted him for his money.

"I'm sorry if I overstepped the mark. I just wanted to help."

I wriggled toward him. "I know, and I'm sorry for snapping. I just don't want people to think that I'm only with you because of the money."

"I don't care what people think."

"If that were true we wouldn't be keeping this a secret."

Neil slid his arm under me, pulling me close. "The last few weeks have been frustrating. I've seen you shine with your work, and your boss claim all the credit. It's not fair that someone so talented has that taken from them. I didn't mean anything by it, Nicola. I just know how tough you and your parents have had it."

"And I appreciate that, but it's not your place to help me. Can't we just enjoy this right now?"

He smiled, and part of me regretted how harsh I'd been.

Maybe the way he'd come out with it was wrong, but his heart had been in the right place. It was as much my decision as his to keep us secret.

"Of course. I didn't mean to upset you."

I was lost again as his lips grazed my neck and I closed my eyes, shutting out the world. Nothing else mattered in that moment but Neil and I.

I'd make the most of it while it lasted.

ELEVEN

WE WENT from zero to a hundred after that, unable to get enough of each other. Most nights Neil would be at my place, and the week went by so fast, it was the end of the following week before I knew it. Which meant one thing.

Lunch with the girls.

Rebecca was acting weird. Part of me had thought that she might have found out about her father and I, but she didn't say anything. Plus, she was still friendly with me.

It was her dietary behaviour that was odd.

She abandoned salad for our monthly lunch, going for that juicy, fatty steak yet again. My mouth would water, but the additional cost put me off.

The steak might be tempting, but my car still needed a service.

It was Friday, and I'd taken the afternoon off. When I'd finished at the restaurant, I headed to Neil's place. He'd been asking me to visit and stay the night with him for a while. I think he wanted to sleep somewhere other than my small bed with the hard mattress.

Nothing had changed. I smiled as I drove up the driveway, looking around at the immaculate gardens, the huge front lawn. This was a place for children with so much room. Sadness hit me as I realised the only child he'd had here was Rebecca, and she was usually elsewhere.

His house was the castle he'd built for his princess.

I'd spent time here as a teenager, of course. The four of us were quite often at Rebecca's place because we didn't want to be home. The last thing I'd wanted was for my friends to find out we had very little money. Katya's parents could be cold and distant and barely tolerated her at times, let alone three extra teenagers. Gemma's parents were always tripping around the world somewhere. So for me, Rebecca's house was home.

I hadn't been here in years. It was a single-level house, but big. I shivered at the memory of their big spa bath. We'd never been allowed to use it when we were kids. I looked forward to soaking in it now.

My heart beat like crazy as I knocked. Despite us spending quite a lot of time together, this was still so new and so naughty. Our little secret. This weekend, we'd be inside our little bubble without anyone disturbing us.

Neil grabbed my hand when he opened the door, pulling me inside and into his arms.

"You took your time."

"If I go rushing from lunch with the girls, they'll know something is up."

He kissed me, his lips pressing hard against mine, and I relaxed into him as his tongue found my own.

"Like that, is it, Mr Wallace?" I asked with a laugh.

"Always, with you." He held my hand, pulling me toward the hallway. "Come on. I've got something to show you."

"I've seen your house."

"Not this bit."

Right down the end of the hall, behind a door that had always been closed when I had visited, was Neil's room. It was plainly decorated, with grey walls and what looked to be a king-sized bed.

"So, the first time I've been here in years and the first thing you want to show me is the bed. I'm beginning to think I'm only here for one thing." I gave him the most wide-eyed, innocent look I could possibly give him.

He smiled. "I'm assuming you have some bag with you, unless you're going to wear the same clothes all weekend. Although ..." He sighed. "You could wear nothing all weekend."

The grin spread across my face before I knew it. "Yes, I've got a packed bag in the car. I was in such a rush to get inside, I forgot it."

"This is what I wanted to show you." He pulled open a drawer in one of the dressing tables at one end of the room. It was empty.

My pulse quickened, and I clapped with delight. "You're giving me a drawer? That seems awfully serious."

Neil crossed the room, taking my hands in his. "I wanted to show you how serious I am. I love all the sex, don't get me wrong, but there's more to us than just that."

I flung my arms around his neck, and he laughed as I covered him with kisses.

"Does that make you happy?"

"It makes me very happy. I will accept your offer of a drawer. Unfortunately, my bedroom is too small to have spare drawers, so I can't offer you a reciprocal one."

He laughed again and shook his head. "I guess it just means we'll have to spend more time here."

"Aren't you worried Rebecca will find out?"

Wrapping his arms tight around my waist, he pressed his lips to mine in a moment so tender my insides turned to mush.

"Rebecca rarely visits. Most of the time when we see one another it's in a meeting, or we'll have lunch or dinner in town. The likelihood of her coming here and discovering us is very, very small."

My heart ached for him. He'd tried so hard, but clearly they weren't close. All my memories of Rebecca involved a sometimes sad, rebellious woman who loved her father very deeply. If I knew that, why didn't he? The gulf between them was obvious, and having come into this knowledge, I needed to find a solution. One which, for the moment, didn't involve her finding out that I was her father's lover.

"She loves you." That was all I managed, but it was enough to get his lips to curl into a small smile.

"I've no doubt she does. She suffered through my breakup with her mother, I know that, and I also know she hated how hard I worked. But everything I ever did was for her."

I licked my lips, taking in his sad demeanour. "I know enough to know she misbehaved to get your attention."

He sighed. "How about we stop talking about my daughter, and talk about us? I thought we could spend time relaxing, maybe have a bath, and I'll cook dinner."

"That sounds perfect."

Neil's eyes lit up. "Good. I've freed up the weekend, so I thought it would be a good opportunity to really get to know each other. I don't know where this is going, but I know I want more."

"So do I," I whispered.

He pressed his lips to mine again, lingering as he let me go.

"We're in agreement, then."

"I guess so."

I couldn't help the grin across my face. Simply being with him did that. I'd never been with a man who made me feel good all of the time. I didn't have to try to be anything but myself around him. It felt like forever since I'd been able to do that.

THE SPA BATH was every bit as amazing as I'd imagined. I sat in bubbles almost up to my collarbone, closing my eyes at that wonderful feeling of soaking in the warm water.

"You look content," Neil said, slipping into the water behind me.

"This is so relaxing. Just what I need."

He wrapped his arms around me. "You're what I need."

I leaned back against him. "It's nice to be here. I thought we were going to spend every night squished into my bed."

He laughed and planted gentle kisses on my neck. "My bed is bigger and softer. I don't know how good your bed is for my old back."

I twisted, turning to face him. "I like that bed."

"I bet you like mine better." He grinned and leaned in, brushing my lips with his. For a moment we gazed at each other before he kissed me again, deeper, longer.

Neil ran his hands down my sides, and I giggled at the touch. "Ticklish?"

"A little."

He dropped his hand down between my legs, stroking my clit. "Ticklish there?"

I flopped my arms over his shoulders. "I don't know if ticklish is the right word." A warm flush rolled over me, and it wasn't the water.

Neil watched my face intently, his eyes lighting up as I let out a long loud breath. I closed my eyes, leaning against his body, the water moving as I thrust my hips toward him.

"Nicola," he whispered. I opened my eyes to see him gazing at me, with a small smile on his face. "You're beautiful."

Kneeling, I moved closer, over his lap, lowering myself onto him. I gripped the edge of the bathtub, moving my hips slowly as he pulled me down, his mouth claiming mine as I claimed his.

He moaned and I picked up the pace, the water splashing over the top of the tub and onto the floor. I laughed, holding his shoulders tighter. He tensed, sucking gently on my neck as he dropped his hands to my hips, pulling me hard against him.

His lips found mine again, and I cried into his mouth as he gave one last thrust inside me, groaning loudly. Panting, I pressed my forehead to his.

"If this is what taking a bath with you is like, I may never shower again," he said.

I laughed. "I have plenty of shower ideas."

The look of affection he gave me as I pulled away brought a flicker to my heart. I sat beside him, and he slipped an arm around my waist.

"I think I could eat a horse after that effort. What's your favourite food?" he asked.

"I get my favourite?"

"After that, you can have anything you want." He laughed.

"Spaghetti and meatballs."

Neil frowned. "I don't think I have that, but I'm sure I can conjure up something."

"Pretty sure those magic hands can do anything." I waggled my eyebrows.

I could never get enough of this—the bond we were creating between us. But the closer we were, the harder it would be if either of us had to walk away.

I had fallen hard with no intention of stopping.

TWELVE

I STAYED the following Friday night too.

Telling my boyfriend we wouldn't be spending Saturday night together was one thing. Telling him the reason why—because I had a weekend planned with his daughter—was another. We'd discussed it at our previous group lunch date, and Rebecca had decided tonight would be the night.

How the hell did I end up in this position?

The thought made me smile. What other positions were there that I hadn't explored with Neil, and ...

That's enough.

For the first time in my life, I had someone who wanted me for me. Neil told me I was beautiful, loved my body, and didn't care what I wore. I could be myself with him.

But going public was a big step, one I didn't know we were ready for. Once we went public, I wouldn't have to lie anymore. To myself or anyone else.

Neil sighed in his sleep and rolled over to face away from

me. I wasn't the only one who had benefitted from this relationship. According to him, I'd brought the peace to his life he'd always craved.

We were so good for each other. The hard part would be convincing Rebecca of that.

I didn't know what the time was, but it was way too early to be awake on a Saturday morning, and I snuggled up to Neil, spooning him, using the warmth of his body to avoid the chill. These were the best times—the quiet moments when I could enjoy being with him without stressing about anything else.

He stirred, rolling back toward me, a half-asleep smile on his face.

"I thought you were fast asleep," I said.

"Your toes are cold." He laughed, throwing his arm over me.

"Sorry."

He gazed at me with so much affection it was clear he shared my feelings. "I'm getting used to it."

I nestled against him as he stroked my hair, raising my face to meet his for a kiss.

"I like waking up with you," he murmured.

"I like it, too."

"Want some breakfast? Or is it too early?"

I rubbed my nose against his chest. "I just want to stay here a while longer."

"Anything you want."

"I'm staying at Rebecca's tonight."

Neil's eyebrows crept up. "What?"

"She suggested a sleepover a while ago. Like the old days.

All the girls will be there."

He smiled. "Sounds great."

I pouted. "I thought you might miss me."

His smile grew into a grin, and he planted a kiss on my nose. "I will. You and your cold toes."

"It's just one night. I promise I'll make it up to you."

His eyebrows waggled as he laughed, flopping his arm over me. "I look forward to it."

KATYA WAS ALREADY at Rebecca's when I arrived, her late-model BMW parked in the driveway. I parked my car out on the road. Rebecca lived in a decent neighbourhood; it'd be alright there for the night.

I knocked on the door. Laughter floated out through the open windows, and I patted my hair down nervously as I waited for Rebecca to welcome me in.

Panic gripped me. What if Rebecca could smell her father on me? We'd spent most of the morning in bed making up for me not being there for the night. Had he hugged me after showering and getting dressed? Did I smell of his cologne? *Shit.* Had I used his spray-on deodorant? I'd done that a couple of times before going to work when mine was AWOL.

Rebecca opened the door with a smile, and hugged me as we stood in the doorway. "Nicola, it's so good to see you. Katya's already here, and I'd like you to meet my friend Olivia."

Phew.

Clearly I didn't smell like her father. *What an idiot. Keep it together.*

I stepped inside, and into a warm reception. Katya shrieked and ran to hug me, and I shook my head at the very pregnant Olivia pushing herself up off the couch.

"Don't you dare stand up." I grinned as relief swept her face and she eased back down.

"It's not really that bad," she said.

"Doesn't have to be. Tonight is for pampering ourselves. Besides, if I damaged you in any way, Logan would never forgive me." Rebecca laughed.

Olivia rolled her eyes. "It's bad enough that he thinks I'm made of china."

"You can sit back and not do a thing," Rebecca sat on the couch beside Olivia, motioning for me to sit. I occupied a recliner chair opposite and sank back into the soft leather.

"What have you been up to?" Katya asked me.

I shrugged. "You know. Same old. Work and home. Rinse and repeat."

"Sounds boring."

An image flashed through my mind of Neil pinning me to the bed as he made my body hum. Katya and Rebecca had already turned back toward Olivia, but as I let out an audible sigh at the memory, Katya's head snapped back and one of her perfectly formed eyebrows was off the charts.

"What? It's just nice to relax," I said.

Rebecca's smile grew. "I think tonight will be great. Give us all a chance to do just that."

She seemed so happy, happier than I thought I'd seen her in a long time. Was there something specific causing that? My stomach ached at the thought of shattering that bliss. It had to happen at some point.

What was I going to say to her? *"Hey Rebecca, I'm screwing your dad."* Wouldn't that just go down well?

Lost in thought, I jumped when a knock interrupted my daydream. Rebecca rushed to the door to open it, and on the other side stood Gemma, a bottle of wine in each hand and a grin on her face.

This was going to be a long night.

A LOT of wine and one soppy movie later, we were all a mess on the living room floor. Tissues were everywhere as we bonded in some drunken cry-fest. Olivia, who obviously wasn't drinking, sat on the couch, bemusement etched across her face. What a great introduction to our little group.

Somehow, we ended up on the topic of our sex lives. Everything was a bit hazy from the alcohol, and Katya started talking sex. It was always her who began these conversations, usually bragging about her amazing sex life with her fiancé, Tim. I suppressed a groan at the thought of hearing about that, but we had to talk about something. Why not one of the few things we'd been talking about since we were in our late teens?

"So that's no sex for Gemma, lots of sex for Katya. What about you?" Rebecca looked straight at me.

A sea of expectant faces looked back as I scanned the room, my cheeks searing. Dare I say something? I wanted to burst with everything I felt for Neil. I didn't have to reveal his identity, did I? Thinking about him made me all warm and fuzzy.

"Well, I met someone."

"Who?" Rebecca asked.

"He's older. Quite a lot older. I had a crush on him a long time ago, but recently we ran into one another and something just clicked." I sucked in my lower lip, keeping my gaze on Rebecca. She had such a big smile in her eyes.

"So? Tell us all about him." Gemma broke through the moment.

I shrugged. "There's not that much to tell. We're enjoying spending time together."

Gemma rolled her eyes. "No. Tell us about the sex. You know, for those sad sacks who aren't getting any. Right, Rebecca?"

An uncomfortable expression flashed across Rebecca's face. Her lips quirked before she straightened up and smiled. "Yeah, right." She had something to hide too, but the others missed it. I saw the look in her eye.

My heart thumped as I took a deep breath. Might as well jump right on in. These were the people who I'd shared so much with over the years. We weren't as close as we had been back when we were in school, but this whole evening was a chance to rebuild the tight friendship that kept us coming back together once a month for our lunch. These were my friends, and I'd never had a problem talking about my sex life with them before.

I licked my lips. "Oh. That's amazing. I was really worried that the image I'd built in my head would turn out to be a load of crap and that the sex would be boring, but that is not the case."

"Really?" Katya's eyes grew wide. Just like that, my anxiety disappeared. None of them would put two and two together. By the time Neil and I told Rebecca about our relationship, maybe she would have forgotten what I was saying tonight. We were drinking.

I couldn't help myself. "He can go for hours, and he's huge—like crazy big." My grin was from ear to ear, and the urge to grab my phone and call Neil just to hear his voice swept over me. The wine gave me tingles, and thinking of him and our many intimate nights left me with a warm buzz that I wanted to hold onto forever.

"Lucky girl." Katya smiled.

"Sounds great, Nicola. I'm really happy for you." Rebecca raised her glass. "To amazing sex and good friends."

Katya turned her attentions to Olivia, and the spotlight was gone from me. Now I'd spoken up my nerves got the better of me, and I gulped down the wine in my glass, grabbing another refill. The girls didn't notice. They had moved onto someone else's sex life. My secret was safe for the meantime, but my head spun with what I'd just said.

Why on earth did I have to go into that much detail?

Even if it was all true.

THIRTEEN

I SKIPPED GOING HOME after Rebecca's and went straight to Neil's place, driving straight into the garage. He smiled as I walked in the house, kissing him on the cheek while I walked through and dropped my bag on the bedroom floor.

"Have you had breakfast? I can make you something," he said, as I flopped down on the couch in the living room. I had looked forward to spending Sunday with him, but I had zero energy.

"Rebecca cooked bacon and eggs. They're surprisingly good when you have a hangover." I covered my face with my hands. My head ached, and more sleep was in order.

Neil's footsteps disappeared into the kitchen and then returned. "Here."

I pulled my hands away and opened my eyes. Neil stood over me, a glass of water in one hand, two painkillers in the other. "Here, take these and drink all of the water. I'll get you another glass, then you can go back to bed."

"You're so good to me." I sat up, taking the pills and water. I gulped down the liquid as the drugs slid down my throat. It had been a long time since I'd been this hungover. I'd forgotten just how awful it was.

"You should have had a big glass of water before you went to sleep."

I shrugged. "Then you wouldn't have to take such good care of me."

His lips curled into a smile, and he leaned over to give me a kiss that was so tender when I closed my eyes, I struggled to open them again. "Maybe I like taking care of you. I'll just get you some more water and we'll get you off to bed."

"I don't know; it's pretty comfortable here. If I close my eyes again, they might not re-open for a few hours."

His chuckle was the last thing I heard as I did just that, drifting off in the knowledge that I was safe and cared for. *All I ever wanted.*

When I woke, my head was still hazy and my stomach grumbled, protesting at not having had anything to eat since breakfast. The curtains were drawn, and through the tiny gap I saw the sky had darkened.

My nostrils filled with the scent of meat cooking and tomatoes. *Yum.* My mouth watered.

I sat up, rubbing my neck as I orientated myself. Whatever Neil had cooking smelled amazing, and I stood, walking into the kitchen to find him stirring a pot.

"You're awake," he said with a smile.

"I guess I slept all day."

"I thought you might get up and go to bed. The couch is comfortable, but the bed would be better."

I shrugged. "I think it would have taken a tank to drive through the living room to wake me up. What are you cooking?"

"Your favourite. I figured after a big night and being asleep for the day, you'd be hungry when you woke up."

Wrapping my arms around his waist, I leaned my head against his back.

"If you start snoring again, I'll try to catch you before you fall over." He laughed, leaning his head back.

"What do you mean again?"

DINNER WAS MAGNIFICENT, and Neil smiled as I took a second helping. I never took a second helping.

"Good then?"

"Amazing." The word was muffled by me taking a mouthful of meatball. I hadn't been so hungry in my whole life, and I knew I'd sleep well tonight even after my marathon nap.

I stacked the dishwasher when I was finished and switched it on. This place was like home now.

Neil sat on the couch and flicked on the television.

"I had a random idea. A client of mine offered me a couple of tickets to his new paintball business. I was going to offer them to my staff, but how about we go?" He grinned, showing off those perfect teeth behind those perfect lips I loved kissing.

"I've never been paintballing." I sat beside him.

"Neither have I. Problem is that these are only good for during the week. So I thought that if it's enough notice, you could maybe take next Friday off work and we could go. Then we could share a long weekend together."

Placing my hand on my heart, I stared at him in mock horror. "You, the great over-worker, Neil Wallace, taking a whole day off? Whatever will people think?"

He leaned closer, the affection clear in his eyes. "I don't care what people think. My life has changed so much with you in it. I want to embrace it, live it to the fullest I can."

"That includes shooting balls of paint at me?" I stifled a giggle. "Whatever turns you on."

Neil waggled his eyebrows. "You do." He pounced, pinning me to the couch, unleashing the giggles I'd been holding in as he kissed my neck.

This man, this impossible man, so hard to resist and yet all kinds of wrong for me. Rebecca might not be the only one who reacted badly to us being together. My parents, though living an unconventional life, could be very old-fashioned when it suited them. It might just be Neil and I against the world.

Could he handle that?

Could I?

Again, I pushed all rational thought to the back of my mind as I reached for my panties, sliding them down before pushing them off with my feet. We were about to defile the living room sofa, and I didn't care. I'd sat here in my teens watching movies with my friends, and now for the I-didn't-know-how-many time, Rebecca's father was about to be inside me.

This was my internal conflict. The battle between right and wrong raged in my head, but as he leaned over and went down on me, I sighed.

My vagina overruled everything yet again.

But it wasn't just that particular part of my anatomy that melted when he showed just how much he wanted me. My heart clung on just as fiercely.

Oh holy crap. There it was. Warm waves rushed over my body as the sensations this man made me feel grew, and I sighed as I was engulfed in a swirling tidal pool of arousal and emotion, carried away by my thoughts, completely unaware of him pausing.

"Are you okay?" His lips twisted in confusion.

"Very okay."

IT WAS with great reluctance that Renee gave me Friday off. It wasn't like we were that busy, and I had the time owing, so she gave in with a grimace. Now I sat in Neil's car, the breeze blowing through my hair. My bag sat on the back seat beside his with my spare clothing to change into once the 'fun' was over.

I'd never seen the appeal of running around shooting people with paint, but if it meant a whole extra day with him, I'd do whatever he wanted.

For his part, I'd never seen him so relaxed, wearing a polo

shirt and track pants, and sporting the evil smile of a man up to no good.

"How bad is this going to be?" I asked.

"How can it be bad? I get you for three whole days."

My cheeks burned, the way they always did when he paid me a compliment or told me how much he wanted to be with me. Our 'thing' wasn't new, but I couldn't remember the last time I'd felt so wanted by someone.

"I don't think I've seen you completely without makeup. In the mornings, you usually have the remnants of the previous day. Even when you were going to school, you lot used to wear it even when you weren't supposed to." My heart froze, and he glanced at me twice before frowning. "Have I said something wrong?"

"No, of course not." In one of those moments I thought I'd managed to leave behind, prickly heat traversed my body. Was he disappointed that I didn't look my best? Shit. I was so comfortable with him that I hadn't thought of it. I was used to getting up early to put my face on, although lately I'd gone to bed without washing it off. It was hard to shake the habit of feeling guilty for not making the effort.

"You look beautiful, by the way, if that's what you're worried about. I don't think I can resist that face, whether it has make up on or not."

I exhaled loudly and grinned. "I figured I'd be covered in paint soon enough."

Neil laughed. "I could be a lousy shot yet."

We pulled up to a huge shed with a sign that said "Paintball Heaven" on it.

I rolled my eyes. "Seriously? They couldn't come up with a better name than that?"

Neil laughed. "Ignore that. Come on, you keep saying you miss working with paint."

"Yeah, to paint. Not for it to be shot at me, or shoot."

Uncertainty crossed his face. "We don't have to do this if you don't want to."

"It'll be fun. I'm just being silly. I've never done this before."

"Neither have I. We don't have to do it for long, and then I'll take you home for lunch and wine."

I nodded. "Now you're talking."

With increasing trepidation, I approached the building. This would be fun, but for who?

Inside, we were dressed in overalls and protective chest gear. I pouted as I put the goggles on to protect me from hits in the face. "Who's going to shoot me in the face?" I asked, thankful none of my friends were here. All these years building an image would be wasted if they could see me now.

"Hopefully no one." Neil looked as stupid as I did.

Paintballing had never been on my list of ideal dates. As we walked out into the main playing area, I looked around, noticing for the first time how empty it was.

"Is it just us?"

He laughed. "We're the first people here to play. The place actually opens tomorrow. We helped these guys out with business finance, so they were kind enough to let me take an early look."

"I have no idea what I'm doing."

"Neither do I."

With a grin, we parted ways. The place had rock-type formations to hide behind, and with only two of us, I had my doubts about finding Neil to shoot at.

For around five minutes, I stalked, imitating the cops in those TV shows where they sneak around corners to find the gunman.

Smack.

I hadn't thought about how much it would hurt to get hit, and the pain spread from the spot on my neck that had just been targeted. It stung and I put my hand to where it hurt, the pain wetting my fingers as I probed the tender spot. That would give me a nasty bruise.

"Gotcha." Neil laughed.

"I thought you were supposed to aim for around here?" I danced around, waving my arms and pointing at the bits of my body that were protected.

"I did. I never said I was a good shot." He drew closer and frowned as I went back to rubbing my neck. "Are you okay?"

"I'll be fine. It's just my ego and this spot on my neck that'll bruise." I kept rubbing my neck, rubbing the painful spot again.

He smiled, cocking his head. "When we get home, I'll kiss it better."

"Promises, promises. Want another go?" I laughed. "Payback is going to be a bitch."

Neil looked thoughtful for a moment, his smile spreading into a grin. "You're on."

As he backed away, I picked up my gun and aimed it at his thigh. He cried out as the crimson paint splattered on his pants.

"I'll kiss it better later."

He laughed, despite franticly rubbing the spot, ducking behind a wall so we could continue our game.

This wasn't over by a long shot.

I'D NEVER LOOKED FORWARD SO MUCH to the spa bath at Neil's place. My legs ached from running, my arms ached from holding the gun, and in the visor mirror on the drive home, the bruise was already coming out on my neck.

"I think a nice long spa bath and a bottle of wine will help us feel better," Neil said.

"That sounds so good. Let's order pizza, too."

He laughed. "That sounds even better." He flicked a glance at me. "Did you enjoy today?"

"Loved it. I don't think I've laughed so much in forever." I snuggled into the car seat. "I'll sleep well tonight."

"I was kind of hoping neither of us would get much sleep this evening."

I grinned, watching him as he drove the rest of the way back to his place. Today had been fun, despite my initial reluctance, and it had been good for him. I was good for him. We were good for each other.

For my part, I had stopped being so anxious about the way I looked. I'd even gained a bit of weight over the past months and not flown into a panic about it. Neil liked me for me, and his company was what I craved now.

Our relationship was unlike anything else I'd ever experienced. By now it was clear he wanted more than sex, and that was what I wanted too, but how far could this go?

I slipped off my shoes inside the door and ran for the bathroom. Neil laughed as I twisted the taps and slipped my shirt over my head. "That anxious for a soak?"

"Aren't you? I think every muscle in my body aches."

He grinned. "I think I'm in better shape than you."

"That wouldn't surprise me."

I slapped his hand as I dropped my bra on the floor and he reached for my breast. "That's for later."

"I'll go get the wine."

Turning my head, I pecked him on the lips. "You do that."

Slipping off my pants and underwear, I stepped into the bath. It was at ankle level, and I swirled the water around with my feet, mixing to get a good temperature. It just made the urge to sit in its depths even stronger. This had to be the best part of the day.

As I sat, letting the water fill the tub around me, I pondered the day. I had my doubts that activities like paint-balling were a regular part of Neil's life. In the time we'd spent together, this was the most radical thing he'd done. I liked it.

I closed my eyes, the warm water getting higher, and took a deep breath. This was the life. Twisting the taps off, I leaned on the side of the tub.

"Dad?"

My stomach lurched as I heard the familiar sound of Rebecca's voice.

I froze. The bathroom door was partially open, and if

Rebecca came too far down the hallway she'd find me naked, sitting in the spa bath.

"Dad?" she called.

"Rebecca? What are you doing here?" Neil asked, the warmth for his daughter obvious in his voice.

"I thought I'd call in. Your PA said you'd taken the day off. I thought I'd better check up; it's so unlike you." She was so close. She had to be at the entrance to the living room, right near the hallway.

"Aren't I allowed to take a day off once in a while?"

She laughed. "Says Mr Workaholic." Her voice grew more distant, and held my breath. She must have gone into the living room.

"I'm fine. You don't have to worry about me. Don't you have work to do?"

"I might be playing hooky too."

Shit. She wasn't about to leave. What the hell was I supposed to do? Especially if she wanted to use the bathroom.

"Dad, what did you do to yourself?" Rebecca's tone changed as she cried out.

"Oh, the bruise. I got it playing paintball."

"What on earth were you doing playing paintball? And why didn't you invite me?" There was a hint of hurt in her tone, and I wondered if Neil had picked up on it, or whether he thought she was just being bratty.

"I'll invite you next time. Believe me, this was payback for hitting someone else. I'm not the only one nursing a bruise."

The conversation had died, and I strained to hear what might be going on. Footsteps drew closer, and I held my breath as the bathroom door opened, letting it out when Neil slipped through the door and closed it behind him.

"I'm so sorry. She hardly ever visits like this," he murmured.

"She was clearly worried about you."

He nodded. "I tried to hint for her to go, but she's sitting at the kitchen table." Neil swallowed, hard. "Maybe it's time to tell her about us."

"Katya's wedding is in a month. I wanted to get that out of the way so I don't put a downer on it." I sighed. "You need to spend time with Rebecca, and if she's here to check up on you maybe I should just leave you to it. I don't want her to find out this way."

"You don't have ..."

"I'll get out of the bath now and get dressed. If you keep her talking, I'll grab my bag from the bedroom and sneak out the front door. I can get a taxi home."

He shook his head. "That's not fair."

"I'll be fine. Just call me when you're ready." I slowly stepped up and out of the bath, grabbing a towel from the rail and wrapping it around me. "Give me five and I'll be out of here."

Neil gripped my chin, tilting my face toward his and looking at me with those beautiful blue eyes. "You really are one in a million." He dipped his head, kissing me softly. "Rebecca's going to think I've died in the bathroom. I'll come 'round when she's gone. Sorry we didn't get our nice relaxing evening."

I shrugged. "It's par for the course. I'd rather we organised a get-together to tell her than her finding out this way."

Neil kissed me again and slipped back out of the bathroom. I sighed, drying myself off with the towel, and pulled my clothes on quickly.

Her laughter floated through the house as I sneaked out the bathroom and into the bedroom where my bag lay on the bed. I tiptoed to the front door, breathing a sigh of relief as I spotted my sneakers in the shoe rack just inside the entranceway. How Rebecca had missed my bright pink shoes, I'd never know, but I picked them up quietly and slowly opened the front door.

On the other side, I took deep breaths of the fresh air, calming my anxiety. What the hell was I doing? This was right up there on the crazy scale for me, but I walked down the driveway and into the street anyway, stopping when I got to the end of the road and taking my mobile out of my bag.

I called for a taxi, and I leaned against a nearby fence in the sun while I waited for my ride to appear, all the time stressing about what to do if Rebecca appeared.

How long she'd visit her father for I didn't know, but I did know that this was what he needed. If all of this mess could somehow bring the two of them closer together, that had to be a good thing.

But given the way we'd been sneaking around, I might never get her forgiveness.

I had to be prepared for that.

***

"WE NEED TO TELL HER." They were the first words out of Neil's mouth when he showed up at my apartment later.

I'd wavered so many times between wanting to tell Rebecca and being terrified of losing her and even her father. Panic gripped me. "I'm not ready."

He grasped my arms. "Nicola, it doesn't matter when we tell her, she'll still react in some way."

Tears welled in my eyes and I blinked them back in a vain effort to stop them. "I ..." I swallowed hard and let out a sob. "I don't want to screw up Katya's day and if Rebecca and I fall out, that's exactly what will happen."

"I know you're scared, but I'm right here. I'm not going anywhere."

"That's what you say now. What if she goes nuts about us?"

He let go of my arms and enveloped me in a huge hug. "I think you know you're more important to me than that."

"You're important to me, too. So is Rebecca. And Katya."

"There's still a month to the wedding."

"And that means I get one more month with my friends before it all blows up in my face."

His grip loosened and he scanned my features. "I love how you care so much about your friends. I just don't want a repeat of today. That was horrible for you."

I shrugged. "You're here now."

"Let's go back to my place. It's not too late for a soak and a good night's sleep."

My lips cracked into a smile, despite the tears lingering on my cheeks. "As if we're going to get a lot of sleep."

"You know me too well, Miss Crandell."

FOURTEEN
ONE MONTH LATER

IT WAS the Friday before Katya's wedding, and I felt like crap. Even though I'd had plenty of sleep, I was exhausted, nausea hitting me in waves. Dragging myself out of bed, I went through the motions, managing to get to the end of the day without Renee yelling at me too many times. All I wanted to do was crawl into bed.

I had plans to spend the weekend at Neil's place. Rebecca hadn't been back since that day we'd gone paintballing, and I looked forward to the peace and quiet with that we'd enjoyed the past month.

"You look like shit. Maybe you're pregnant." Tamara's charming words echoed in my head as I sat on the bus, heading to the supermarket and then onto Neil's place. I looked down at my phone to check the time, noticing the current date. My period was late, but that wasn't unusual, given my flirtation with extreme weight loss.

This time, however, a nagging feeling in the back of my

head grew. Being late, combined with feeling gross—I could be way off the mark. Tamara was joking, it was a thing she said to everyone, but what if the two things were linked?

I walked up and down the aisles at the supermarket, picked out a few things for the weekend, and in the aisle with the sanitary items, I picked up a packet of tampons and with my paranoia getting to me, a pregnancy test. Just to make sure.

My phone buzzed as I got back in the car. *Stuck in a meeting. Will get home as soon as I can. Don't cook, I'll bring something home.*

Home

I'd come to see that house in such a different light these past few months. It was disappointing to go to my place again, back to my tiny flat. Everything about his house was luxurious. It made me a little angry at Rebecca's rebellion. She'd had everything. Although, I also carried the guilt that her father had spent more time with me lately.

They both deserved more.

I parked my car in the garage. At least on the off chance Rebecca did turn up, she wouldn't see it. We'd held off telling her at my insistence, but this subterfuge was really getting to me now. At least the wedding was in two days and we could tell her after that.

Inside the house, I placed the groceries I'd bought in the kitchen, slipping the tampons into my bag and taking the pregnancy test to the toilet. No time like the present to put my mind at peace.

Three minutes later, there were two lines.

Two freaking lines.

I sat on the toilet, cradling the test in my hands, my head spinning as I counted those two little stripes over and over again. It didn't matter what I did, there were definitely two of them.

"Shit."

Neil would go nuts. Here we were both thinking this couldn't happen. All these months we'd been having unprotected sex, thinking nothing ever could. But clearly it had.

A few years ago, in another lifetime, I would have given anything for this moment. Now I was scared, uncertain how my partner would take it. He was in his fifties. Would he want to start a new family?

Another thought struck me. I'd had so many false alarms in the past. What if this was just another trap to fall into? Before telling Neil or anyone else, I had to get a blood test done. The more I thought about it, the more I doubted the strip in my hand.

What a mess.

Tears rolled down my cheeks as I continued staring at the test. What about Rebecca? I'd have to confess to what I'd been doing either way and the thought of hurting her stabbed me in the chest. I'd come so close to telling her when we'd had that sleepover. Why couldn't my life ever be simple?

"Nicola?"

Neil calling my name woke me out of my stupor. I sniffed, wiping my eyes with a piece of toilet paper. "Just a minute." My voice shook, but would he notice through the wall?

Taking a deep breath, I stood, sticking the test into my

pocket and giving my eyes a final wipe. I blew my nose and threw the paper into the toilet, flushing.

I opened the door and made my way through the house looking for him. "Neil?"

"In the kitchen."

He stood at the bench unwrapping a giant parcel of fish and chips. As I drew closer, he turned his head and smiled. "I came past the fish and chip shop on the way home, and thought about how long it's been since I had these on a Friday night. Used to be the family tradition. Well, mine and Rebecca's tradition."

"Smells amazing." I wrapped my arms around his waist, burying my face in his back. He was warm, familiar—everything I'd come to associate with being home.

"Are you okay?" He leaned back on me as he scooped handfuls of hot chips, and the two pieces of fish onto plates.

"I'm fine. It's just been a really long week."

"Renee working you hard?" He scrunched up the paper, rolling it up to go in the bin. I let go of him, opening the cutlery drawer and pulling out a couple of knives and forks.

"Something like that. It's the weekend now. Time to forget all of that for a little while."

Neil turned, a plate in each hand. "Let's do that. Did you want a glass of wine with your dinner?"

"I think I'll just grab a soft drink. I don't feel like wine with fish and chips." I laughed. We often had a wine with dinner. I wouldn't be able to skirt around that one for long. I needed time to get my head around it, and my uncertainty about how he'd take it wasn't helping.

"Grab two," he said as he disappeared into the living

room. I stood for a moment and took a deep breath. My head was already crammed with thoughts about what to say to Rebecca, how to tell her that her father and I were together. Now this.

"Nicola?"

"Coming." I called, grabbing the cans of drink from the fridge and making my way to the living room. Neil sat on the couch, loosening his tie, the two plates on the coffee table. He slipped out of his jacket, throwing it on a nearby chair, and smiled as I sat beside him.

"Hungry?" he asked.

"Ravenous. I'm so glad it's Friday." I opened my can of drink and took a long sip as he took the other lemonade from my hand.

"Me too. I've been thinking a lot about Sunday." He looked at me, pausing. "Erica called me. She wanted to know if I could take her to the wedding."

My stomach rolled, and I narrowed my eyes. "I can't go with you, but your ex wants to?"

"She's by herself and really wants to go. She was good friends with Katya's mother in the past."

"You said yes."

He placed his can of drink on the table, turning toward me. "It's not like I'm taking you. That was your decision."

Tears welled in my eyes and I slammed the can on the table, the lemonade spraying around. "I know, but of all the people to take."

"Nicola, things have been over between Erica and I for years. You know that. I'll take her, she can talk to her friends, and then I'll come home to you."

My lower lip wobbled. If they were going to get back together, it would have been years ago. I had nothing to worry about and I knew it. It didn't make it hurt less.

"You're the one I want to be with," he said, so gentle and sweet.

"I know. I'm just being silly."

"No, you're not." Neil pulled me into his arms. "We're both still adjusting to the idea of being together. Getting serious is a big step for both of us. We're going to have speed bumps." He kissed my temple. "Now, let's get to this food before it gets cold."

He let me go, picking up the television remote to flick through the channels, settling on the news before picking up his plate. He'd taken a handful of paper napkins through, and he handed me one with a smile as he began to eat his dinner with his fingers, breaking the fish apart.

"I'd forgotten how good this was," he said.

I smiled. This brought back memories of my own family life. We had our own Friday night tradition, and I suffered pangs of guilt at how long it had been since I'd seen my parents.

Picking up my plate, I nearly inhaled the food. I hadn't realised how hungry I was until the fried goodness was in my mouth. It had been so long since I had eaten anything like this, full of fat and salt. Delicious.

"Good, isn't it?" Neil said with a laugh. "The shop down the road is amazing. The couple running it have been there since Rebecca was small. Everything's so fresh."

"It's amazing."

"You're eating like you haven't had anything for months." He laughed.

"I'm enjoying it. There have been times in my life when I've almost forgotten how good food can be. Gotta make the most of it."

Neil smiled. I knew he worried about me. Over the past few months I'd confided in him, told him all my deepest secrets, shared my darkest fears. I'd been friends with his daughter for around seventeen years, and he knew more about me than she did.

I couldn't give him up. Wouldn't.

I welled up. Stupid hormones. He put his plate down and took mine from my hands. I felt safe when he wrapped his arms around me, and we sat there in silence as he just held me.

"Are you okay?" he whispered after a few moments.

"It's been a really long week. I'm tired and cranky and looking forward to being able to be with you in public."

He was so sweet. He stroked my hair and planted kisses on my cheeks to remove the tears that rolled down them, all without pressing me further or giving me a hard time about the delay in telling anyone being by my choice.

I loved him.

FIFTEEN

KATYA'S WEDDING. *The* event of the year, and the thing that had hung in the air over Neil and I while we bided our time in telling Rebecca about us. After this, we'd sit her down and talk to her. As a couple.

Neil didn't say what he would do if she flat-out rejected me, and I didn't ask. If the time we enjoyed together now was all we had, then I was determined to make the most of it.

I went dateless. There was no point stringing someone along for a day, and my closest friends were already going. Of course Neil and Erica would be there, too.

Rebecca's mother had a drinking problem. As much as Rebecca loved her, she'd had her fair share of being the grown-up in their relationship. I didn't remember a lot about Erica other than when Rebecca stayed with her, we usually weren't invited around.

"I promised I would help her out. She wants desperately to go." His words hadn't helped, even though I was the one

wanting to hold off telling Rebecca. For just one night, my three best friends and I would be united and enjoy each other's company. After that, who knew what would happen.

I could lose everything.

I drove into the car park of the church where Katya's wedding was being held. Up by the building, Rebecca stood, talking to her parents. My stomach clenched at the sight of Erica with Neil, jealousy raging in my veins. I could do nothing, but at least Rebecca looked happy. She was by herself too.

Not far from them was her ex-boyfriend, Alexander, and his fiancée, Clarissa. Alexander's focus, however, was completely on Rebecca. He'd cheated on her, and she'd dumped him. Up to that point, they'd been so good together, and sometimes we talked about him a little too much for her.

Now the woman he was going to marry was completely oblivious to her man not paying attention to anything but his ex. She looked around the gathering crowd as he stopped and stared.

I shifted my focus back to Neil and found his eyes locked on me. The depth of warmth in them made my heart beat faster, and I looked away to stop the moment, even though I didn't want to. Being apart from him at this moment was torture. Torture of my own making.

Swallowing it down, I took a deep breath and smiled when I saw Gemma heading my way. On her arm was a tall, good-looking guy. So one of us had managed to bring a date.

"Nicola. We're just going into the church. Want to come and sit with us? This is Justin, by the way."

I nodded. "Sure. I'll just be a minute. I want to catch up with Rebecca first."

Shifting my gaze back to Rebecca, I raised my eyebrows at the sight of Alexander and his lady approaching her. I cringed at the thought of how that conversation would go.

Gemma and Justin were already on their way into the building, and I took a step toward it myself, only to spot Neil coming out a side door.

"What are you doing?" I asked as he approached me.

"Back this way," he said, turning the way he'd come.

Behind the church was a group of trees. Everyone was out front, and no one would notice us there. As I walked behind him and out of sight, he grabbed hold of my arms and kissed me. It wasn't just a polite 'I'm so glad to see you' kiss—it was a passionate, aching kiss of need.

"I hate not having you on my arm," he whispered.

"I hate seeing you with *her*."

"It's just for today. I'll be with you tonight."

I nodded as he cupped my cheek with his palm. "We should go. The wedding is going to start soon." He brushed his lips with mine, lingering for a moment before he broke contact.

"Right behind you," I said.

Sighing as he walked away, I touched my fingers to my lips. Every single one of his kisses was burned in my memory. This whole time I'd been on a precipice, wondering when I'd fall and lose everything. Whatever happened, I had the kisses, and a child growing inside me I hadn't yet told him about.

I shook my head to try shake that feeling for the moment.

Katya's wedding was what I had to concentrate on, not mooning after my lover who was with his family.

Before heading inside, I pulled my phone out of my bag and checked it for the billionth time. My doctor had been reassuring, but had advised waiting for a blood test to confirm any pregnancy given my previous hormonal problems. Waiting for the results was torturous.

There was nothing, so I turned toward the door and walked inside.

To my horror, everyone was seated in the church, and Katya's car had pulled up outside. I slipped in the door, spotting Gemma and Justin sitting with Rebecca. Today, that was where I belonged.

I squeezed in with my girls and waited for Katya to come in. As her sisters walked the aisle first, I giggled to myself. She had chosen the most wishy-washy shade of beige, fading them into the background.

Katya appeared, and I gasped as she approached. I couldn't have designed anything as lovely as she looked. The fading light through the stained-glass windows cast a rainbow over her white dress. I dug desperately in my bag, pulling out a tissue and dabbing as my eyes welled up with tears.

On the other side of the aisle sat Neil with Erica. I caught his eye, and he gave me a quick smile before turning toward the bride and groom, now getting ready to exchange vows.

I flicked a glance at Rebecca beside me. She was focused on Katya and didn't seem to have seen a thing. I didn't know what hurt more—hiding this from her, or the knowledge that our friendship would likely soon come to an end.

This was way too hard.

THE MARQUEE where the reception was held had me sweltering, and I escaped into the fresh air as soon as the dinner was over and dancing begun. As the night grew darker, it was easy to hide away where no one could see me.

Neil found me.

"Hey, beautiful," he said as he drew close.

I looked around. No one was near, and I sighed as he took me in his arms and kissed me. "Hey, yourself."

"Have you had a good time?"

I nodded, hugging him tight. "The wedding was beautiful. I wish I was with you, though."

"Soon, nothing is going to keep us apart." He kissed the top of my head, and I eyed up the big, old house next to the marquee.

A wicked thought occurred to me, and my raging hormones weren't helping. If I lost him after we told Rebecca, this could be our last chance to be together. An overwhelming urge to be naughty for perhaps the final time overwhelmed me. Whether I could talk Neil into it was another matter.

While most of the guests were in the big tent, there were a few hanging around the building. There had to be a deserted room there somewhere.

"Do you think there's a spare room in there?" I tried to concentrate as Neil nuzzled the spot below my right ear.

"Why? What did you have in mind?" He chuckled.

I pulled away. "You, me, somewhere in there ..."

His eyebrows twitched with uncertainty. "I don't know …"

"Where's Erica?"

"Talking to Katya's mother I think. At least, that's where she was a few minutes ago."

"I hate you being with her. You're mine."

His lips twisted into a half smile, and I knew I almost had him. The thought of losing him if Rebecca rejected me cut to the quick. I needed him.

He sighed. "Nicola, you know I want to be with you."

I slipped my arms around his waist, pressing my body to his. "I want you so much right now."

"I hope you know how hard it is to resist you," he whispered.

He was hard against me, and I slipped my hand between us, touching him through his pants. Tilting my head, I ran my tongue along his jawline until I reached his ear.

"Shit."

I had him.

"Go inside and see if you can find a room. I'm not in any condition to be among people."

That brought a grin to my face. "I'll be back in a few minutes."

"Don't take too long."

I kissed him softly and ran toward the house. A handful of people milled in and out. The catering company had cooked all the food in the kitchens inside, and the serving staff still went back and forward to the marquee, serving drinks.

A long corridor that seemed deserted hung off the side of the large front room, and I ventured down it, looking around to see if anyone had noticed me. The rooms going off it seemed to be used for storage, and I smiled as I got to the last one. This was perfect. It didn't look as if it had been touched for a long time, and we'd be away from the crowd and anyone likely to find us.

The more I thought about it, the more I wanted him. Here and now. No one would ever know but us.

I looked around as I came back down the hallway. No one as much glanced at me, and I made my way back behind the marquee where Neil waited.

"I found the perfect spot. There's some storage rooms that don't look like they've been touched in ages. Everyone is busy or drunk. They'll never notice us."

He pulled back a little as I grabbed his hand. "I'm not so sure ..."

"Now."

His lips curled into a crooked smile. "You want it that much?"

"That much."

I let go as we got to the corner of the marquee. "I'll go first. It's the corridor off the front room. Right down the end on the right."

He nodded as I left again, my heart beating so fast I thought I would pass out before I got there. Standing by the door was Clarissa, Alexander's fiancée. I barely glanced at her as I walked past, but noticed she stood alone.

I opened the door and slipped in, taking another look around the room. There were folded chairs in the corner gathering dust. Maybe they only got them out for extra large weddings. It was clear they'd been there a while.

The door clicked, and I turned to see Neil. He closed it behind him gently, and crossed the room, taking me in his arms. His lips were warm and welcoming, and he kissed me as if he hadn't seen me in a hundred years, even though it had only been a few minutes.

"This is so ... I don't know ... You make me crazy," he whispered.

"We need to be quick. Just in case."

"There's no lock on the door."

"So hurry up." I grinned, reaching up under my skirt and pushing my panties down. I stepped one foot out of them and waited.

"Lean against the wall." With a zip he undid his pants, and I turned toward the wall, placing my hands on it for support.

He moved behind me, slipping his hand around me and between my legs, his fingers working their magic as I ground against them. With his other hand, he pushed my hair from my neck, taking big mouthfuls of my skin.

"I love it when you do that," I moaned, steadying myself.

"Bend over a little."

Without any more words, he drove into me as I positioned myself better, and once he was inside me I straightened up a little, bracing myself against the wall as he pushed me up and off my feet. I fisted my hand, biting down on it, trying not to make any noise. This was so naughty, so dirty. Neil's ex-wife was just outside in the marquee, and here he was inside me. Because he was mine.

"I don't think I can actually take any more today." Rebecca's voice came from the doorway, and in an instant, Neil pulled out of me and stepped back.

With a thud, I hit the floor and I scrambled to pull up my panties, hanging around one ankle, as he spoke to her. She sounded calm, but I think that was just because she was pretty drunk. Her voice was flat, lifeless, and she looked straight at her father, ignoring me as she asked him to take her mother home.

She closed the door as she left, and Neil bent to help me up. "I'm so sorry, Nicola."

"It's not your fault." I took his hand, letting him pull me to my feet. "That wasn't supposed to happen."

One side of his mouth curled into a crooked smile. "No. It's my fault. We took a risk. I'm supposed to be the sensible one." He sighed, running his fingers through my hair. "I just can't keep my hands off you."

I slid my arms around his neck. "You know I feel the same way."

"Guess it's my fault for having an insatiable girlfriend." He pecked me on the lips. "I'll get Erica home and see you at your place? Or do you want to go back to mine?"

I shrugged. "Doesn't really matter now, does it? Your bed is more comfortable. I could do with a spa bath, too. Anything to relax after that. What about Rebecca?"

He sighed. "I'll talk to her in the morning, try and smooth things over. I don't want to make things worse by pushing her."

I squeezed him tight, and he relaxed into me. I'd have to work out how to tell him about the baby. But this wasn't the time or place to dump that on him. He already had a difficult relationship with Rebecca; I'd probably just made it a million times worse.

This sucked. I loved them both.

"See you at my place then. If I'm quick enough, I might just be able to catch you in the bath."

"I intend to be there for a while. This is going to need a really long soak." I tried to keep things upbeat, but inside I was in turmoil. Rebecca could hate me for this; Neil could dump me for her. But I couldn't resent her for that. What would I do if I walked in on my father with one of my friends?

He looked at me for what felt like the longest time, not saying anything, just taking in my features, almost as if he'd never see them again.

"I'll see you soon." The kiss he left me with was so tender, and as he exited the room first, I put my fingers to my lips.

I waited a few minutes, just to make sure no one saw us leave the same room. All I could think about was Rebecca's tone. What was she thinking?

We were an odd bunch. Katya the organiser, Gemma the pretty one, Rebecca the rebel and me, the artistic one. But we all cared so much for one another, and during the last few months I'd especially admired Rebecca for breaking out of her box. Since I got together with Neil, I'd felt like a rebel, too.

Now everything could be over. If I hurt Rebecca that badly, how would the others react?

I took a deep breath and pulled open the door. I'd go and retrieve my bag from the table and get out of here. The thought of that bath was inviting. It might be the last time I got to enjoy it.

Clarissa, Alexander's fiancée, was farther down the hallway. She looked at me with an eyebrow raised and I wondered just how much she'd seen of the whole fiasco.

"If you're looking for Rebecca, she went that way. So did her father." She smiled sweetly, and I swallowed down the urge to rip her throat out. I'd no idea why—she just rubbed me up the wrong way. Maybe it was because when Rebecca and Alexander were together and he wasn't screwing around, they'd seemed so happy and in love, and I thought that just maybe one of us would have a happy ending.

"Actually, I'm just off to get my bag and go home. It's been a long day."

"And a busy night."

She knows. Damn it.

"How is your night going? Where's that boyfriend of yours got to?" I smiled just as sweetly. With Alexander's track record, he was probably off trying to score with one of the bridesmaids.

"He's around somewhere. Not too far, I'm sure."

Yeah, I bet you keep him on a real short leash.

"Oh well, have a good night. Don't let him wander too far."

I walked away, spotting Rebecca on the veranda. Alexander stood there too, and I slowed as he moved closer to her.

Oh, don't you dare.

No way would she go down that particular rabbit hole

again. I glanced back over my shoulder at Clarissa, standing in the centre of the room and looking around. It looked like she was trying really hard not to look like she was searching for Alexander, but seeing as she knew no one else, that was all it could be.

I took a step off the veranda and across to the marquee where my handbag was.

"Nicola." Katya's warm tone sounded like at least she was happy to see me.

Now what?

Katya came rushing at me, flinging her arms around my neck.

"Hey." I laughed.

"Rebecca blew Tim."

I gaped at her. "What? When?"

She waved her hand. Her eyes were glassy from too much alcohol, and her words were slurred. "I don't know. Years ago. When they were at uni. But neither of them told me. I am so pissed."

"Why?" It was a genuine question. If it had been when they were at uni, it was at least seven years ago. Katya had been with Tim for two.

"Because they didn't tell me."

I slipped my arm around her waist as she looked at me, her eyes so sad. "It was forever ago. Believe me, Rebecca loves you, and I'm pretty sure Tim likes you too."

She smiled, raising her hand which up until her marriage had one big glittery ring. Now there were two. "He does, doesn't he?"

"He adores you, Katya. I bet he just didn't want to hurt

you. Would you have let him get this far if you'd known early on?"

Her internal struggle was obvious as she twisted her mouth. "I guess not. Maybe. I don't know. You're right."

"I'm always right. Didn't I tell you dressing your brides-maids in beige was the right move? You looked incredible, by the way."

She hugged me tight and took a deep breath. "You're right. I need to go and talk to Rebecca. Say sorry for the drink I threw at her."

"You go do that. And then enjoy your wedding night with the man you love. Have wild, crazy sex and an amazing honeymoon."

Katya kissed me on the cheek. "Are you still seeing older guy? If not, we'll have to find a nice man for you next."

I nodded. "Sure thing." No point in complicating things even further.

I watched as she climbed the steps, approaching Rebecca. Hopefully that little situation would sort itself out. Things were bad enough as it was.

Locating my bag, I walked out to my car, sitting in the car park. Under the cover of having to drive, I hadn't had a drop to drink and I sat in the car for a moment, holding my hand to my stomach, warmed by the life that grew inside me. What-ever happened between Neil and I, this baby had been conceived with love.

Tonight, I'd just go to his place, soak in the bathtub and sleep in that big, soft comfy bed. I'd already taken the next day off work—even without drinking, it made sense after a late night.

The car spluttered to life. Its service was still overdue. That was just one of many things that I'd put off because it cost too much. Only now it was likely to cost even more from my neglect.

If Neil and I went public, people would think I was with him for his money. Nothing could be further from the truth. I was used to living off the smell of an oily rag. We'd done that enough at home.

I drove through the quiet streets contemplating everything that had just happened. What would I do if Neil broke up with me? Go back to my boring life, working for mega-bitch Renee? I just couldn't picture my life without him, though. These past few months had meant more to me than anything ever had.

I love him.

We'd skirted around it, but never said the words. All I could do was hope he felt strongly enough about me to fight.

I pulled into his driveway and fished the front door key out of my bag. The door opened with a click, and I pressed the buttons on the alarm, entering the alarm code Neil had given me.

I loved this house. He'd never shared it with Erica; he'd moved here after they'd split. This was the place he shared with me.

Home.

Hell, it might as well have been for all the time I'd spent here.

I threw my bag on the couch in the living room and made my way toward the bathroom, twisting the taps to get the water going. While it was filling, I went into Neil's bedroom to grab some of my things.

In the drawer were a couple of changes of clothing, some spare panties and a nightie. I grabbed some panties and the nightgown and left them on the end of the bed while I returned to the bathroom.

Smiling, I grabbed a bottle of bubble bath from the cupboard, pouring in a generous amount to give me lots of bubbles. I sat, watching the tub fill, swishing the water around with my hand until it was up to my breasts. The bubbles smelled fruity, fresh, lightening my mood.

I'd give anything to know what Rebecca was thinking.

That night at her sleepover, I'd very nearly told her about Neil and I. I almost wished I had. Then I could have borne the brunt of her anger and got it all out of the way.

I was so happy for Katya—happy she'd got the wedding she wanted. Those two would live happily ever after. I was sure of that. At least I had that to keep me smiling, even if it felt like the rest of my world was falling down around me.

Lost in thought, I barely heard footsteps falling beside the bath, and looked up to see Neil smiling down at me. "You look comfortable."

"It's nice. Get in and stop me from thinking too much."

He laughed, unfastening his tie and throwing it on the floor. I leaned back in the bubbles closing my eyes until I felt hands on my shoulders.

"Move up."

"There's plenty of space in here."

"I know, but I want to sit behind you."

I wriggled forward and he stepped into the bath, wrapping his arms around me and pulling me back to lean on him.

"What a day, huh?" He nuzzled my neck.

"You could say that. Are we okay?"

Neil stopped. "Do you think I'd be in this bathtub with you if we weren't?"

"But, Rebecca ..."

"Rebecca's a grown woman. Tomorrow I'll go and talk with her. She loves both of us, Nicola."

I sighed, running my fingers through the bubbles. "I know, but this is huge."

"She's going to have to get used to it."

I raised my hands to grasp his, wrapped around my waist in a hug. Relief flooded through me. I didn't know if I could give him up if I had to. "What if she doesn't?"

"Rebecca has a big heart. She and I might not have the closest relationship, and I know she's done things I probably shouldn't have approved of, but I let her carve her own path. I hope she's mature enough to do the same for me."

Tears pricked in my eyes. The fear of Rebecca rejecting him growing as I snuggled back against his body. He might say all this now, but what would happen if tomorrow she told him she wasn't happy about our relationship?

"Move in with me," he whispered.

I pulled his arms off me and turned to face him. His eyes were full of uncertainty, but warm as always. "Are you ready for that?"

"Would I have asked you if I wasn't?" He raised his bubble-covered hand to my face, and I wrinkled my nose as they burst, splashing my cheek. Running his thumb down to my lips, he ran his gaze across me until he met my eyes with a smile.

I swallowed hard. "I want to."

"Then, move in." He made it sound so simple when a million reasons not to ran through my head. But there were two things that trumped them all.

I loved him, and I was carrying his child. I opened my mouth to say something, but closed it again. Not until I knew for sure.

One thing at a time.

"I will."

SIXTEEN

FOR A WEEK I'd been frozen, barely moving other than back and forward to work. I spent the days just going through the motions, as I couldn't think of anything other than the flat tone of Rebecca's voice when she'd found us.

Neil had seen her since, and she'd been 'wonderfully understanding' according to him. Would she be so forgiving of me?

I hadn't officially moved into Neil's place yet. This thing with Rebecca hung over me, and yet I couldn't get up the nerve to make contact.

Neil was his usual caring, considerate self. He gave me the space to work things out without applying any pressure. By the following Sunday, I just wanted to get it over with, and he was spending the days this weekend at a finance conference.

It took a while to work out my mobile was ringing. From

the bottom of my handbag, the sound it made broke through the silence.

I dug through the bag, scrambling to answer it in time. "Hello?"

"Hi, is this Nicola?"

"Yes it is."

"This is Lorna from Doctor Anderson's office. I've got your test results. Sorry it's taken so long to call, we've been understaffed and very busy."

I swallowed. "That's okay."

"Your blood test confirmed your pregnancy. Do you want me to make an appointment with Doctor Anderson to discuss maternity care?"

My heart leapt from my chest. After everything, the disappointment of thinking I may never fall pregnant to finding love with a man who had finished his family as far as he was concerned. This was not the outcome I'd expected.

Tears streamed down my cheeks, and I closed my eyes.

"Hello?"

Crap.

"Sounds good. Please make an appointment."

"What time suits you?"

"I have lunch at twelve. Any day." Some part of me still couldn't believe what had just happened. As scared as I was at the prospect of telling Neil, I'd held onto the hope that this was real.

It being real was thrilling.

"There's an appointment available on Wednesday if that works for you."

"Yes please," I whispered.

I needed more than ever to reach out to Rebecca now. Not only did I want her to forgive me for what had happened at the wedding, I needed her advice on how to handle this with her father.

"See you then," Lorna said brightly, and I hung up the phone and stared at it for a moment.

> I really need to talk to you. Are you at home today?

I pressed send.

Closing my eyes, I wondered if she'd call me at all. What would I do in her position?

> Everything's fine. Don't worry about it.

It would have been so easy to just leave it, but I would still worry. I needed her on my side, somehow. The baby growing in me was her half-brother or sister. I typed another message.

> Tell me when you're home and I'll come over. I really do need to talk.

> I'll be home after lunch I think. I'll text you.

Great. Only another few hours of torment. I lay down on the couch and flicked on the TV. The TV news droned on and on as I stared at the ceiling.

I couldn't stay in one place and slipped back off the couch, wandering toward the laundry where I found the vacuum cleaner. Neil had told me that I needn't do any of the cleaning, he had someone come in to do it, but that wasn't me.

Lord knew what I vacuumed, the floor was clean to start with, but there was something soothing about the repetitious nature of the task and it took up a bit of time.

Not enough.

I went back to the couch and lay down, closing my eyes. A little nap wouldn't hurt, and this past week had been tough to get through. I'd been so tired.

My head was still in turmoil, going over everything that had happened the previous weekend. Despite that, it didn't take long to hit that sleepy state, where I was so close to nodding off. I shook with a jolt as my phone buzzed on the table and I picked it up.

My stomach churned at the sight of Rebecca's text message, the words *I'm home* scaring the crap out of me. Facing up to Rebecca was terrifying, but I had to do it. I couldn't leave Neil to deal with any fallout.

I let out a big breath. It was now or never. I couldn't ignore the situation even if I wanted to.

It was a short drive to her house and I sat in my car outside, gathering up the courage to go in. What was the worst thing that could happen? She could reject me as her father's girlfriend, and drive a wedge between us if we let her do it. Hurting her was the last thing in the world I wanted to do, but I couldn't change the way she'd found out.

I closed my eyes for a moment. I had to be brave. Summoning all my courage, I got out of the car and walked to the door. When she answered my knock, Rebecca's expression was neutral.

"If you think I'm going to yell at you, I'm not. Did you talk to Dad?" She stepped back, and I walked past her and into the living room. The last time I'd been here, I'd got carried away, telling her and my other friends about this wonderful older man I'd been seeing.

"I spoke to Neil. He said you were fine with us. I just wanted to be sure."

She sat beside me.

"I'm not going to cause a fuss. You're both adults. Who am I to even try to interfere?"

"I love him, Rebecca. Really love him. I spent so long worrying about what this person and that person thought of me. Starved myself to be thin, ate to put on weight. When I'm with him, I just feel like I can be myself." I looked at her hopefully. Surely all the times she'd shown she cared about my health meant something.

"You don't need to justify yourself to me."

I let go of a huge breath in relief. She still sounded neutral, but at least she wasn't angry.

"Nicola, what is it? Clearly there's something else going on."

I licked my lips, trying to get moisture to my mouth. At the thought of telling her about the baby, my tongue felt like sandpaper. "I'm pregnant."

Her jaw dropped a little.

"It's your father's. He's been the only man I've been with for months, but I know this could put extra pressure on us." My voice got squeakier as I spoke, and I picked at my fingers like a teenage girl.

"What do you think I'm going to do about it? Make you

get rid of it? Tell him to leave you? If you know him that well, you'll know he'll not want to walk away. He tried so hard with my mother because of me, and then he tried without her to take care of me."

Tears welled in my eyes. I'd expected the worst, and while she didn't come out and say she approved, her letting things be meant so much. Especially in my hormonal state.

I sniffed. "The day of the wedding—I am so, so sorry you walked in on us like that. I just have these wild, crazy raging hormones and when I want it, I have to have it. Neil is so accommodating like that."

Rebecca rolled her eyes. "See, that's the bit I don't want to know. If you love him, fine. If you have sex with him, fine. But I don't want to know about it. That's all I'm going to ask of you. Please don't tell me more stories about how big my father's penis is and how well he uses it."

I couldn't help myself. I got the giggles and laughed as she shook her head.

"For him to sneak off like that with you in that kind of place speaks volumes for your sex life. I really don't need any more details."

My emotions overwhelmed me and I threw myself at her, hugging her tight. "Thank you. I never wanted to hurt you. And when we were kids I never thought your dad was hot. But oh God, Rebecca."

"There's a line, Nicola ..."

"Sorry. I keep saying sorry. Shit. How am I going to tell him about the baby?"

She pushed me away. "What? You haven't told him?"

"I only had it confirmed today. I've tried a couple of times to tell him, but I'm so scared in case he doesn't want it."

Rebecca reached for my hands "I saw his face when he told me about you. He loves you. He'll probably want to do the right thing and whatever you want. Just be good to him."

I grinned. "That's the easiest thing to do in the world."

I DROVE BACK to Neil's place. There was nowhere else I wanted to be but with him right now. Besides, it was time to tell him about the baby, given that I'd told his daughter.

Rebecca hadn't exactly given our relationship her blessing, but she wouldn't stand in our way. She'd even dealt with the baby news way better than I'd imagined.

How would her father take it?

I slid my key into the front door lock and turned. The door opened into that gorgeous entranceway with the polished wooden floor. This place was so beautiful, and yet Neil had asked if I had any suggestions to improve it. Like he wanted me to put my touch on his house.

I unset the alarm and made my way toward the bedroom. At least now I'd had the conversation with Rebecca, my stress levels had dropped. I could go and take a proper nap.

Sinking into the large, soft bed, I yawned, and sleep took hold before I knew it.

When I woke, the clock said it was nearly five p.m. and Neil wasn't due back until around seven. I transferred myself from the bedroom back to the couch in the living room, and watched TV while snacking on potato chips.

Bored with the television, I switched it off and sat up on the couch in the silence, staring off into space as I thought about what would come next.

What would he think? Would he want a DNA test to prove it was his? Clearly his vasectomy hadn't worked properly all those years ago. But would he believe it?

How did my life get so complicated?

The living room light flickered on and I blinked, surprised at the bright light. Neil chuckled, dialling the dimmer to soften the glow.

"Sorry if I gave you a fright. I didn't see you there in the dark."

"I lost track of the time." I tried to smile, but my lips wouldn't quite do what I wanted them to and I had to force them up at the corners.

He sat beside me, pulling me into his arms and planting a kiss on my temple.

"How was your day?"

"I saw Rebecca." I took a deep breath, snuggling against him.

"You should have told me. I would have come with you."

I shrugged. "She was fine. I mean, she seemed okay. Just laid down some rules around sharing information."

Neil reached for my face, tipping my chin toward him to look into my eyes. "Sharing information?"

"She doesn't want to hear about our sex life."

He laughed, kissing my cheek. "I think that's fair enough."

I leaned in, taking a deep breath, inhaling that clean shirt smell. *I love him.* I loved this man so much.

"Are you okay?" He stroked my hair, resting his chin on the top of my head.

"There's something I need to tell you." The knot in my gut grew, and I resisted him raising my head again, looking down at his chest.

"Nicola, look at me. What's wrong? Was it anything Rebecca said?"

I shook my head. "No, she was lovely. Nicer than I deserved after what happened at the wedding."

"Then what is it? How can I fix it if I don't know what it is?"

I sat up straight, steeling myself to look him in the eye. "I'm pregnant."

His face went blank. I'd have given anything to know what he was thinking, but then again that might not have been the greatest of ideas. This was the last thing he'd expected.

"I don't understand." His voice cracked.

"Neither do I, but it happened." I wiped away the building tears, blinking to try to stop them coming.

"But I ..."

"I know. You had a vasectomy. And I've not been with anyone else."

His eyebrows knitted together as he scanned my face. "I know that. I wouldn't have asked you to move in if I didn't trust you. This is completely ... unexpected." He sounded calm, just as he always did, not giving anything away.

"It was the last thing I thought would happen. I mean, I always thought maybe I'd have children one day, but I'd gotten used to knowing that I probably wouldn't."

"Oh, Nicola." Now he sounded pained, as if he'd been wounded. *Was he about to let me go?*

"It's not like my apartment is leased to anyone else yet. I don't have to move in."

"Don't you dare."

My breath hitched.

"I asked you to move in and I meant it."

"But the baby ..."

He shook his head, his facial expression softening. "I have no idea how to process that right now, but I'm not prepared to let you go that easily. Do you not realise just how much I love you?"

I was a mess of tears, throwing my arms around his neck and holding on tight.

"Hey," he murmured.

Sniffing, I smiled through my teary eyes, letting go and cupping his face in my hands. "I love you too," I whispered.

"So, it's settled. You move in and then we work out where to go from here."

"Does that mean you want me to get rid of it?" That was the next fight. I was thirty years old and there might not be any more opportunities. If he didn't want the baby, I had that decision to deal with. The ache in my stomach gnawed at me with the knowledge that this last hurdle might still break us up.

"Did I say that? My head is still spinning, sweetheart. Let me catch up."

"I guess something didn't work properly?" I shrugged.

He grinned—*grinned*. "Sounds more like it did."

I slapped his shoulder gently. "Are you actually proud of yourself?"

He laughed. "Honestly, I don't know what's up and what's down. I had that vasectomy twenty years ago. But then again, the only woman I ever gave up condoms for was you."

He took my hands in his, looking at me with so much love that I wanted to cry some more. "In all this time I've never had such a serious relationship. I never thought I'd find love again, but you ... you're perfect."

I shook my head. "I'm far from perfect."

"You are to me." He leaned over to kiss me tenderly. "Now. Want some dinner?"

"I should have cooked."

"Nonsense. You need to put your feet up. Do I have to cook a double amount for you?"

I cocked an eyebrow. "What for?"

"Aren't you eating for two? Oh dear God, Rebecca's going to lose the plot now."

Smacking my lips together, I smiled.

"You told her?"

"Today. I told her everything. I told her I was pregnant, and that I love you."

I watched as his face showed a raft of emotion.

"Sounds like this whole 'moving in' thing is settled." He spoke softly, casting his gaze over me with this big, soppy look in his eyes. If he hadn't just told me how he felt, his expression would have given it away.

I nodded. I guessed that was that.

SEVENTEEN

NEXT STOP WAS my parents the following weekend. How they'd take all of this news I had no idea. Me being with Neil was one thing—the baby was another. They'd supported me through my previous attempt to get pregnant with Shaun. Now, I was pregnant to my friend's father.

Maybe things wouldn't be so bad.

We drove up to see them in Neil's car. Dad stood in the backyard as we pulled in, and he smiled and waved, probably recognising the Audi. Neil would have been up here to pick up the painting for his office.

His smile disappeared and confusion grew in his eyes as he saw me, and he flicked a glance between us.

"Nicola, I'm so glad to see you. Did that car of yours finally give up?"

"Not yet." I reached him and leaned over to kiss him on his cheek. He wrapped his arms around me.

"Neil. It's good to see you again. What brings you out here with my daughter?"

I patted his chest. "Dad. We have to talk to you."

"We ...?"

"Just come inside and I'll explain everything."

I led him inside, with Neil following behind. This could have been an innocent trip, but the way my dad reacted implied he knew something was up from the start.

Mum stood in the kitchen and smiled as I came in the door. "Nicola," she said, grabbing me from Dad and wrapping her arms around me.

"Nicola has something to talk to us about. She's here with Neil."

Confusion crossed Mum's face. "Neil?"

"Hi, Marie." Neil spoke from behind me, and my mother shifted her gaze from me to him.

"I was just making us a cup of tea. Would you like one?" Whatever Dad had picked up on had completely bypassed Mum, and she smiled warmly at both of us.

"Sounds great," Neil said.

I made my way into the living room and sat down on the couch. Neil sat beside me, and I held my breath as Dad sat opposite us. We weren't touching, but from the look on his face, you would have thought we were having sex on the sofa.

Mum walked in, placing a tray of mugs on the table.

"So, what do you have to talk to us about?" Dad knew. I could tell from the confusion and hurt in his eyes. And yet my mother still didn't click.

"How's work, love? Are you doing more work for Neil?" Mum asked.

I shook my head. "That's all finished."

"Nicola, what's going on?" Dad asked.

I swallowed hard and focused back on Dad.

"Nicola and I are together." That was all Neil said, but it got the point across. My mother leaned back in her chair, and my father? Well …

"What the hell, Neil? How would you feel if I came to you and told you I was with Rebecca?" I'd never seen Dad so enraged, his nostrils flaring, his hands fisted—the works.

"I would hope that I'd understand. She's a grown woman." He turned to look at me. I nodded, giving him a little smile.

"She's still my daughter. The same one who spent nights at your house when she was a teenager. The same one who has been friends with your girl since they started high school."

Neil nodded. "She is, and until recently, I hadn't seen her since Rebecca left home. That was a long time ago."

"What do you have to say?" Dad looked at me, his dark eyes so sad.

"I love him too, Dad. We're having a baby."

Dad's jaw dropped, and out of the corner of my eye, I saw Mum lean forward.

"It's true. I'm pregnant." I kept my gaze locked to Dad's, and I could have sworn I saw a glimmer of a smile.

"Look, Robert, please believe me when I tell you how much I love Nicola. We're going to be together so I'm begging you, for the sake of your grandchild, please don't cut her out of your life."

Dad swallowed hard, not taking his eyes from me for a second. "This is a lot to take in," he said quietly.

I nodded. "We know it is, Dad. It's a lot for us too. I didn't know when we started seeing each other we'd get so serious. And the last thing I expected was a baby. It wasn't on the roadmap for either of us."

He shook his head before burying it in his hands.

I stood, crossing the room and kneeling at his feet. "You always taught me to follow my heart. It's what I always tried to do. It's what I'm doing now."

Dad dropped his hands, picking mine up from his knees and squeezing them. "I love you so much, Nicola. I only ever wanted what was best for you."

"And you always gave me that. You and Mum and the life we've had. I wouldn't change it for anything. Now I need you to support me."

His lips twitched, and he sighed. "I love you, kiddo. I can't pretend that I'm happy, but I'd never turn my back on you. We didn't give you a conventional life, although it was tempting along the way to conform just to make sure you got everything you needed."

I stood, pulling him up with me and wrapping my arms around him. "I never wanted you to conform."

"Even though we embarrassed you at times?" He kissed the top of my head and my eyes decided right at that moment to leak.

"I didn't know better. I know now. I love you and Mum so much. I don't want to disappoint you."

Dad stood there, just holding me. "You could never disappoint us, sweetheart."

I smelled Mum before I felt her arms around me as she hugged me from behind, that familiar lavender scent filling my nostrils and taking me back to when I was a kid. It had always been just the three of us, but now my heart was that much bigger with the love I had for Neil and this baby would only increase it further.

When Dad let go of me, he turned to Neil. "I don't have to like this, but we'll be here for Nicola and the baby no matter what. I hope you will be too."

"I love Nicola." Neil wasn't budging an inch, and it made me love him even more. He might be trying not to cause a rift, but he was also not going to back away from me.

I sat on the couch beside him, and he took my hand in his and brought it to his lips. The pounding in my chest subsided as an uneasy quiet settled on us. I don't think any of us knew what else to say.

With his other hand, Neil plucked a teaspoon from the tray and added a teaspoon of sugar, he picked up the mug of tea and took a sip. He sighed and leaned back into the couch. "That tea hits the spot after our drive."

Mum sat down. "When's the baby due?"

"I think I'm about six weeks maybe. That's my best guess."

Tears welled in my eyes when she smiled. "A February baby then."

I shrugged. "I guess so. We'll get a better idea in a few weeks when I have a scan."

The atmosphere was still uncomfortable, but Mum seemed to want to make an effort to ease things. Dad glowered at Neil, but my mother lit up as I'd rarely seen her. She'd been by my side when I'd had the tests and been told I may never have children. She knew how much it stung.

There had to be some part of both of them that saw Neil was the right one for me.

"I can't do this." Dad stood, and my heart fell as he turned and left the room. I didn't have to ask where he'd gone. It would be the same place he always went when the world around him didn't meet his expectations. His studio.

Neil rubbed my back as I buried my face in my hands. I knew this would be hard. I was their little girl, their only child. Mum had her own fertility issues having two miscarriages after I'd arrived, and I'd had an amazing childhood with two people who cherished me. I wanted that for my child.

Mum sat on the other side of me, pulling me into her arms. "It's a lot for him to deal with, sweetheart."

"I thought maybe he could be happy that I was happy. It's been so long since I've felt so good."

"Finish your tea and go and talk to him. If I know your father, he'll be throwing paint at a canvas and once he gets that out, he might be a bit easier to speak with," she said, kissing me on the top of my head.

"Thanks, Mum."

"For what it's worth, I'm over the moon about the baby. After everything, Nicola, you deserve to find your happiness."

I met her eyes. They were so full of love and sorrow all at once. "I just hope Dad will end up feeling the same way."

"I'm sure he will. He's got a huge heart, just like you. Does Rebecca know?"

I nodded. "She's okay with it."

"Finish your tea and go and talk to your father. He loves you so much."

Neil's hand landed on my shoulder, and I looked back toward him. He gave me a reassuring smile, and I took a deep breath before picking up my mug and taking a sip of tea. It was soothing, and I closed my eyes.

The last person I wanted to hurt was Dad. We'd been so close growing up and as I'd started playing with palettes and colours, he'd supported me in every way he could. To think of him upset cut me to the core, and yet I'd known he wouldn't just smile and be excited about it.

I drained my cup and stood. Neil grabbed my hand and squeezed it. "You okay?"

"I'll be fine." I reached for him with my free hand and cupped my palm to his cheek. "I can't rewind my life for someone else."

He smiled and turned his head to kiss my hand before letting go.

Leaving him with my mother, who would probably start interrogating him about baby names or some other aspect of having a child, I walked out the back door and toward my father's studio.

Sure enough, he stood in the centre of the room, madly splashing paint on the canvas. This man could paint beautiful detailed pictures, but now he was going to town, venting his frustration.

"Hey, Dad."

The anguish in his face was clear as he turned his head to look at me, and I fought the tears that threatened to overwhelm me at the sight of his pain. We'd been through so much together. A few years before he'd had a heart attack, but he'd fought his way back with Mum and I by his side.

"I know this isn't exactly what you wanted for me, but I'm happier than I have been in years."

"When did this start? Is this why he bought the painting for his offices?"

I took a few steps toward him. "No. I think he bought the painting because I was doing the design work for his decorating project. I think he saw a harmony between your work and mine. Neil wanted the best for his offices, and you and I are the best."

He set down his palette and took a step toward me. "You don't need anyone to validate how talented you are, Nicola."

"It's not his validation that I need. During the project I fell in love with him, and he returned my feelings. That's all there is to it. I chose to keep it a secret because I didn't want to hurt anyone, but I managed to hurt everyone."

Dad shook his head. "You know that's not true. Your mother will be in the markets on Saturday morning telling everyone she's going to be a grandmother."

I couldn't suppress my grin. "She is rather happy about that."

He covered the distance between us and wrapped his arms around me. No doubt he rubbed paint on my dress, but I didn't care.

"I love you so much. If he ever hurts you ..."

"He loves me, Dad. I even gave him an out over the baby and he didn't take it."

"Sweetheart, he is so much older than you." The frustration spilled out in his tone.

"Then we have to make the most of the years we have."

He gave a big sigh. "You're not going to budge on this, are you?"

"Nope. You know how stubborn I am."

"As bad as me."

I laughed. "No one is as stubborn as you."

He let me go as I kissed him on the cheek, and he turned back to look at his painting. "I made a bit of a mess."

"Stick it in a gallery somewhere. Someone will buy it."

"Maybe I should give it to you for the birth of your baby."

My heart fluttered at his reluctant acceptance.

He gave me the smallest of smiles. "My first grandchild."

"I can barely believe it myself. The odds were against both of us, but here we are." I wrapped my arms around his waist. "This doesn't mean you're any less important to me. If anything, our family will be stronger. There'll be more of us."

His chest shook. "You'll be Rebecca's step-mother if you get married."

I rubbed my head on his shoulder. "Be quiet, you."

"It's kinda funny when you think about it."

In that moment, I knew that while he wouldn't be entirely convinced about the strength of our relationship, at least he would support me.

That was all I could ask for.

AS MUCH AS I hated going back to work after being on the high of being free of my secret, Monday was a necessary evil to kick off the week.

I waited until Renee was making a show of being busy before I delivered my blow.

"I need to change my address with you." I held my breath as Renee shifted her gaze toward me.

She shuffled her paperwork. "Send me an email with it in."

"And my emergency contact."

"Did you move?" Tamara asked. "You never said anything."

I nodded. "I moved in with my boyfriend."

"Boyfriend?" Tamara's brows dipped in confusion. I'd managed to keep Neil a secret from her too, even when I was bursting to tell someone. She'd understand.

"I moved in with Neil over the weekend."

"Neil?" Tamara asked.

"Neil Wallace."

Renee froze, her face now set in stone as she stared at me. "Neil Wallace? As in Wallace Finance."

"The very same." At the thought of him I couldn't wipe the grin from my face.

"I'll update my records. Send me that email," Renee snapped, picking up the papers and walking to her office, closing the door behind her.

"Neil Wallace," Tamara said. "I think you have a lot to tell me."

I laughed. "I sure do. Want to go out for lunch?"

"You bet."

She kept looking at me during the morning, and all I could do was smile back. Nothing could touch me—not

Renee and her bitchy behaviour, not the dissatisfaction I had with my work.

At lunchtime, we walked down the road to McDonald's. It wasn't our usual fare, but my stomach grumbled, and I wanted nothing more than to sink my teeth into a burger.

"This isn't your kind of thing." Tamara laughed as we stood in the queue.

"You could say I'm not feeling myself at the moment." I smiled at the lady behind the counter. "Two cheeseburgers and a large fries."

Tamara shook her head as she ordered beside me, and I took a deep breath, inhaling the scent of the food when it arrived.

We sat at a table and I crammed fries in my mouth, barely taking another breath as I ate way too fast.

"You'll make yourself sick," Tamara said.

"I'm so hungry." I looked up at her and grinned. "I'm blaming the baby."

She'd just taken a bite of her burger and started flapping around, coughing and shaking her head.

"Oh my God, are you okay?" I leapt up and patted her on the back as she swallowed.

"What did you say?" she asked as I sat back down.

"I'm pregnant. But only about six weeks, so don't tell anyone. If I get bad morning sickness, you'll notice me disappearing to the toilet a lot anyway."

She laughed. "I'm assuming this is something to do with that little announcement today."

"Maybe." I shrugged.

"So let me get this straight. While Renee had been

hoping to get something going with Neil Wallace, you were scratching that particular itch. Isn't he the father of one of your friends?"

I nodded. "He sure is. We bonded over my designs and we've been seeing each other ever since."

"And you didn't tell me." Her tone was a little wounded. Truthfully, she had been a closer friend to me these past couple of years than my school friends were. She knew of my struggles with money, and how much my weight had fluctuated.

"I didn't tell anybody. The last thing I wanted was for Renee to get wind and be bitchier. Plus, I wanted to give us a chance before Rebecca found out." I took another bite of my burger, and made a mental note to order extra cheese next time.

"That's his daughter, right? How is she taking it?"

I swallowed. "Better than I would have, considering she walked in on us."

Tamara's mouth fell open. "No."

"Yeah, at Katya's wedding. We might have been sneaking around in a back room. But she loves her dad and thankfully she seems to still love me, so we're good."

Tamara flapped her arms around, and I examined her curiously. She couldn't have been choking again; she hadn't taken another bite. "Holy shit. What's Renee going to say when you tell her you're taking maternity leave?"

I leaned back in my chair, my mind going crazy with possibilities. "I don't know, but I'm really going to enjoy telling her."

EIGHTEEN

SIX WEEKS LATER, I chewed my bottom lip, rapping my knuckles on Renee's door.

"Come in."

Taking a deep breath, I let it all the way out before turning the handle and pushing. The darkness of the room hit me as I moved from the brightly lit outer office to Renee's inner sanctum.

"Nicola."

Oh, she was in *that* kind of mood. The kind where even basic courtesy was out the window, and I'd be lucky to get more than monosyllabic words from her. This would be a fun conversation.

Adrenalin rushed through me at the thought of what I was about to give her. Nothing she said could touch me. "I just wanted to give you this."

Across the table, I passed the forms I'd downloaded from the internet to apply for maternity leave. It was early, but I needed her to do her part and fill it in so I'd get anything I was entitled to.

She cast her eyes over it, a smirk growing on her face. "So, you're having a baby."

"I am."

"Congratulations. Who's the father?"

Anger glowered in me. Perhaps I'd been too quick to think that she couldn't get under my skin. "Neil, of course."

She nodded slowly. "I see. You've been seeing him for a while, then." Her attention dropped back to the papers on her desk, and she scribbled notes on a piece of paper with room diagrams on it.

"I have."

"Your design for him was quite different to anything else you've done. Did he help you along the way?"

A heatwave rose up my body and hit my face, my cheeks blazing with indigence. "If you're asking if it was entirely my design, yes it was."

She looked up, fixing those steel grey eyes on me. "Good. We wouldn't want you to breach your employment contract and share designs that weren't yours to share."

I swallowed hard. Technically she was right. I wasn't permitted to show anyone my work outside the company. Before Neil, I'd never done it before, and I hadn't done it since. He was different.

"No, *we* wouldn't."

Let her prove it. Neil would back me all the way. Besides, it was a matter of time before I was on maternity leave and out of this place for at least a year.

I couldn't suppress my smile at the thought of being at

home with Neil and holding my baby in my arms. After everything I'd been through, to be pregnant was the greatest joy.

"I'll get this filled out and filed to the appropriate people." As my smile grew, so did her grimace. Despite our differences, there was a tiny bit of me that felt sorry for her. How lonely she must be, living her bitter life alone.

There was no way she or anyone else would ever make me feel guilty for falling in love. I deserved that happiness too.

It had just taken me until now to see it.

FROM THE DOORWAY of the coffee shop, I smiled as I watched Katya tap her fingernails on the table. Patience had never been one of her virtues, and I was running late after calling her and Gemma to meet me. We hadn't seen each other since the wedding. Katya had been on an extended honeymoon, so I'd had to wait to update her. Rebecca had agreed to leave it to me to break the news.

"About time," she said as I approached. I sat on the empty seat, the one with the lukewarm coffee on the table in front. "I ordered for you, but it'll be cold by now."

"I don't mind. I'm sorry. I had to help someone at work."

"So what's this all about?" Gemma asked.

"I wanted to talk to you two before you found out another way."

One of Katya's eyebrows crept up. "Found out what?"

This was it. There was no easy way to tell them, but at

least they hadn't found out the way Rebecca had. "I've just moved in with Neil. Rebecca's father."

"Moved in?" Gemma asked.

Katya could have caught flies with her mouth wide open. "You and Rebecca's dad?"

Gemma's eyes widened. "Was that who you were talking about at our sleepover? The older guy?"

I chewed on my bottom lip and nodded.

"Holy shit."

I burst out laughing at Katya's words.

"You dirty girl," she said.

I shrugged. "I love him."

Katya frowned. "So how come he was with Rebecca's mother at my wedding?"

I grinned as Gemma took my hand in hers and squeezed. "Because I wanted to keep it a secret. At least get your wedding over and done with before telling the world. I was scared Rebecca would hate me and I'd lose you guys."

Gemma leaned over and kissed me on the cheek. "You would never lose us. We've been through so much together over the years. Did you think we would choose?"

I let out a loud breath. "I didn't know. As it was, I didn't get to tell Rebecca. She found out the hard way."

Katya clapped and laughed. "How?"

"She walked in on us at your wedding."

At that, her mouth fell open again, and it was my turn to laugh.

"We got through that night in one piece. Maybe it was best I didn't know that." Katya patted me on the back. "Do you know what I think we should do now?"

I shook my head. "No."

"Go out for a drink to celebrate."

I let out a squeal and laughed harder. "That is such a great idea, but I can't."

Katya rolled her eyes. "We don't have to get drunk and be out all night."

"I mean I can't because I'm pregnant."

Gemma let me go. "You're having Rebecca's father's baby?"

There was no removing the grin from my face. I hadn't thought they'd turn their backs on me, but two of the people I loved more than anything in the world were right behind me. Sure, my announcement had shock value, but as they sparked a conversation between themselves about the baby news and how excited they were, I knew we would all be okay.

NINETEEN

FIVE MONTHS LATER

PEOPLE SAY that being in a relationship shouldn't change you. That it's a cliché to say you became a better person when you met the one you're with.

I didn't think being with Neil changed me, but having someone who believed in me gave me the inner peace I'd always craved. No more pretending to be something I wasn't. No more lies.

My creativity flourished, and I soon took over a room in his place and set it up as a studio. While I couldn't paint amazing landscapes like Dad, there was nothing more I loved than putting colour to paper or canvas, and then there was the baby's room to style.

Neil protested that I shouldn't be doing so much, but despite that, I decorated it myself. In every spare moment I had, I painted and stencilled patterns until I was happy with the way it looked. It was all done by the time my baby bump had popped out and I grew closer to taking maternity leave.

While all this was going on, I watched Neil fall in love with another girl. She was blonde, frequently wore plaits in her hair, and was four years old. Her name was Ruby.

I wasn't the only one who had kept secrets. Rebecca had been involved with her next-door neighbour, Elliot, on a casual basis. Now it was serious, and Elliot had a daughter from a previous relationship. I loved watching Rebecca take on step-motherhood without blinking.

Neil proudly took on the role of grandfather and looked forward to it a second time when Rebecca announced her own pregnancy.

It was like everything came together at once. Katya clucked around me as I grew bigger, and I didn't have to ask her to know a baby was on the very near horizon for her too.

Even Gemma had settled down as much as Gemma could. She'd moved in with Justin, which was a huge step for her, having lived off her parents for all this time. We were all finally grown up.

I was nearly eight months pregnant and resembled a balloon. Neil loved it, and I often wondered what it had been like for him thirty years before when he and Erica had been expecting Rebecca. We'd sit on the couch in the evenings, his hand on my belly, me snuggled into his shoulder.

The only downside continued to be work. My dissatisfaction with working for Renee grew as I became impatient and tired. I could have given up work at any time—Neil made it clear he thought I should work for myself instead—but I wanted to get my pregnancy out of the way before I did that. Setting up a new business would just increase my stress.

Renee might be a pain in the butt, but I could do the work she gave me in my sleep.

The thought of our first antenatal class scared the hell out of me. I didn't want to think of how the baby had to come out, but it had to exit my body somehow, so it was really in my best interests to go.

Neil was excited about it, just as he found the thrill in every tiny aspect of my pregnancy. Anyone would think he was the one that had to push the baby out.

The classes were at the local library, and Neil drove us after dinner. I yawned, just wanting to crawl into bed and sleep. Not that sleep would be easy.

I had reached the stage where no sleeping position was comfortable, and every time I rolled over I had to negotiate with my body to make the manoeuvre. I'd got to the point where I just wanted it to be finished.

"Tired?" Neil asked.

"I really just want to go to bed."

"It's only for an hour and then we'll go home and I will tuck my princess in. If she's lucky, she might just get some special attention."

I laughed. "I could do with a foot rub."

"I wasn't thinking about rubbing your feet." He reached across and grabbed my hand, pulling it to sit under his on the gear stick.

"That's what got us into this mess."

When we came to a stop, he got out of the car as usual and walked around to help me. Only now, it wasn't just because he was a gentleman—it was because getting out of those soft leather seats was a lot harder with the extra person I carried around.

"Maybe we should have brought my car. It'd be easier for me to get out of."

Neil laughed softly. "Always happy to help."

I kissed him on the corner of his mouth as I stood, holding his hands. "Thank you."

"That's what I'm here for."

I wrapped my arms around his waist, and snuggled into his chest.

"What's this for?" he asked.

"I love you, and I love how good you are to me."

He rubbed my back and I closed my eyes. I could drift off right here in the car park, enveloped in his embrace.

"Shall we move before you start snoring?"

I raised my head to glare at him. "What's with the snoring thing?"

"It's adorable. It's not really snoring, more of a snuffling."

"You're making me sound like a pig."

He chuckled, his chest shaking and disrupting my mini-nap. "My life was so mundane before you were in it."

"I bet it's a laugh a minute now with my cold toes and wriggling to get comfortable in bed."

He let go of me and gripped my chin, tilting my face to look at his. "I wouldn't have it any other way." His eyes were filled with so much love, and a touch of amusement.

"Let's go and learn what to do with this baby. If this pregnancy ever ends," I grumbled.

"You'll be fine," he whispered.

I gripped his hand in mine and we walked toward the

library. An older woman stood at the door, and she smiled as we approached.

"We're here for the antenatal class," I said.

"Just go through; we're nearly all here. I'm Brenda, the teacher for tonight."

"Nicola and Neil."

She smiled. "It's not often we see a young lady accompanied by her father to antenatal classes. It's so nice that you have the support."

Neil gripped my hand tight, but all I could do was grin before giving into the giggles. I turned, burying my face in his body as his chest began to move with laughter. What else was there to do?

When I turned back, Brenda looked between us, uncertainty all over her face.

"Neil's my partner," I said, snorting as I laughed again.

Her jaw dropped, and she slapped her hand across her mouth, clearly mortified at her error. "I'm so sorry, Nicola. I just assumed ..."

"It happens all the time. No one can believe she's so lucky to score an older guy like me," Neil deadpanned, and I slapped his arm.

Brenda shuffled her feet, forcing a smile. "Just make yourselves comfortable. The class should start soon."

We joined a small group already sat on a bunch of chairs in the centre of the room, Neil leaning back and slipping his arm around my shoulders protectively.

"Should I call you dad?" I whispered.

His eyes widened. "Don't you dare. That's just wrong."

All that did was make me giggle more, not helped by the curious stares we were now getting.

"Stop it." He tried his hardest to sound stern, but I couldn't breathe for laughing and I gripped his arm, shaking my head.

"You are incorrigible." I sucked in some air, trying to stabilise myself as he leaned in and nuzzled just below my ear.

"I believe that's what landed us here in the first place," he murmured. Damn it. With my hormones going into overload, I would have done him there and then in the middle of the antenatal class. But that'd have to wait until later.

"Fine. I'll behave." I snuggled back against him, breathing normally until a loud hiccup escaped.

At that I shook my head, clamping my lips together. That was all I needed. I knew the more I laughed, the longer the hiccups would last, so I tried my best to sit quietly as the instructor started the lesson.

To Neil's credit, he sat through a question-and-answer session on everything from breastfeeding to changing dirty nappies and as the instructor spoke, I gazed up at him, watching his complete focus on the class. This was important to him, and for the first time I wondered if he'd done anything like this when he and Erica had been expecting Rebecca.

He shifted his focus to me, smiling as I wrapped his arm around me and held on tight. This was a man who would look after both me and our baby until the end of our days together. I'd never felt so safe with anyone else. So loved.

"Love you," he whispered. He always did know how to read me.

As we walked to the car, he took my hand the way he always did, opening the door for me and making sure I was safe inside before walking to his own side. The perfect gentleman.

He started the car, driving into the street and toward home.

"Did you do any of those classes for Rebecca?" I asked, curiosity getting the better of me.

"No. We had no idea what we were doing. We just learned as we went."

I grinned. "Thank you for coming with me."

"There's nowhere else I want to be. The more prepared we are for this baby, the better. Given how old your boyfriend is."

I leaned over, grasping his arm. "You're the perfect age for me."

We pulled up to a set of red lights and he kissed the top of my head. "All that matters is that we're happy. I don't care what anyone thinks about us."

"That's another thing to love about you."

He smiled, that smile that had doomed me right at the start. "Let's face it—what's not to love?"

I rolled my eyes and laughed as we set off into the night.

He was right.

I JUMPED in the shower when we got home. The weather had been humid, and my clothes stuck to my skin as I sweated up a storm. The warm water added to my tiredness. I knew the second my head hit my pillow I'd be asleep.

Neil was patient. He'd humour me at two in the morning when I would wake up rejuvenated and craving him. The hormones that left me so tired battled with the hormones that made me horny, and the last month in particular had been up and down. If I kept going at this rate, I'd wear him out by the time the baby arrived.

As I stepped out of the shower, I grabbed a towel from the railing and wrapped it around me. The mirror was unforgiving. My eyes were so tired, and I could swear I had the odd wrinkle appearing. Even a year before that would have made me frantic. Not anymore.

The damn towel slipped and fell off, and I sighed, not wanting to bend and pick it up. Instead I took a look at me, how I was now. The same shoulder-length dark hair was there and the same blue eyes, but my breasts were huge in comparison to how they had been and my belly resembled a beach ball.

I ran my fingers over it, the slightly puckered skin where I now had stretch marks wrinkled beneath my fingers. I did have one minor freak out when I first saw them, but given how slight I was and how big this baby was making me, it was of little surprise that I had a couple. Neil would put his hands on them and tell me they'd be a constant reminder of this happy time in our relationship, no matter what the future brought us.

A gentle tap on the door brought me back to reality, and Neil grinned as he entered the bathroom. "What are you doing?"

"Looking at how different I am now. I'm not the woman you ran into all those months ago."

He wrapped his arms around me, pulling me tight against him. "You are, but you're not. You're the same Nicola I fell in love with, but look at you now. You're even more beautiful if that's at all possible."

"Flattery will get you everywhere," I said as he planted kisses down my neck.

"I think it already did." He laughed with his lips over my forehead, his hands stroking my body, and I leaned back against him and closed my eyes.

"You do realise I could go to sleep standing up right now, don't you?"

He stopped and rested his chin on the top of my head. "How about we get you to bed? I'll need to get to sleep as early as possible anyway just in case you decide you want your way with me in the middle of the night."

"I did wrap a towel around me, but it fell off. I'm too fat for it."

Neil turned me around to look at him. "Don't you say that. You're heavily pregnant and gorgeous."

I snuggled into his chest. "I'm happy with myself for the first time ever, I think. I should get pregnant more often."

He walked across the room and grabbed another towel, this time from the heated railing on the other side of the bathroom. When he wrapped it around me, it was warm and cosy. "Whatever makes you happy."

"This makes me happy. All of it. You and the baby and our family. And me. I'm making myself happy."

His eyebrows crept up as he kept his gaze on me. "Are you feeling okay? Have you taken anything?"

"Are you seriously asking if I'm on drugs?" I giggled.

"You're acting like you're high on something."

My face ached from grinning. "Life? I don't know. I think I just found myself."

"Were you lost?"

He slipped his arms around my ever-increasing waist as I snuggled into his chest. "I don't know. Maybe."

"You never have to be lost again."

TWENTY

NEIL CRIED MORE than I did when Noah was born. Birthing had changed since Rebecca was born, and he got to sit by my side through the whole thing, and cut the cord when it was time.

He was the one counting Noah's fingers and toes, and the businessman who had relaxed enough to let our relationship change his life softened again before my eyes.

"He's perfect," he whispered.

"His daddy is pretty perfect, too." I kissed his temple as he leaned in.

"I think it's time to cut back on work, spend more time with my family. I spent so much time working when Rebecca was little that I don't have to this time. All I hope is that she understands."

"She'll be going through something similar soon enough. I'm sure she will."

He passed Noah back to me, and I stroked his cheek with

my finger. My little boy yawned, and then looked at me with those beautiful dark eyes of his.

I'd never held anything so precious in all my life. This was my world back on track. I'd derailed it so long ago, and while Neil was the first piece of the puzzle, Noah was the final detail.

He lined up a photo on his phone and clicked, flicking buttons with a huge grin on his face. "There. Sent to Rebecca and your father."

"Mum's going to freak."

Neil grinned. "They'll see you tomorrow."

"I can't wait."

He ran his fingers through my hair affectionately and bent to peck me on the lips. "In the meantime, try to get as much rest as you can. I'll be here until the ward closes in an hour."

"I want to go home."

"I know, but I'll come and get you in the morning." His phone buzzed, and he laughed when he read it. "Rebecca says she hopes it didn't hurt too much and she'll be up first thing. Ruby's just gone to bed, she'll be so excited when she wakes up to see the photo."

Snuggling Noah close to me, I chuckled. "She's going to go nuts over him. She'll be overwhelmed when Rebecca has her baby."

He had that far-away look in his eyes again, and I didn't have to ask to know he was thinking of his daughter and the grandchild she carried.

"I love the idea that this one and Rebecca's baby will be able to grow up together."

Neil laughed. "I'm looking forward to it. I can just picture two young ones running around with Ruby right behind, instructing them on what to do."

"I think you're right there." I tickled Noah under the chin. "Miss Ruby is going to boss you around; I'm sure of it."

Noah kept on staring at me as we examined each other. My heart swelled with love for this little guy. I didn't think it was possible to love any more, but Noah made me more fulfilled than I had ever imagined. To hold my baby in my arms when I'd once been told I might have ruined any chance I had brought the tears to my eyes all over again.

"Hey." Neil's soft voice broke my concentration, and I leaned against him as he moved closer.

"I never thought I'd get to do this."

"I never thought I'd be doing it again. I'm happy I am, and I'm happy it's with you."

Turning my head toward him, I nuzzled his cheek, kissing him. "I'm glad to be doing this with you. Knowing we'll be there for Noah no matter what."

Nothing could be more perfect about this moment, sitting there with the two people I loved more than anything else in the world.

My family.

OUR FIRST NIGHT was a quiet one. Noah woke a handful of times and I snuggled down with him in the hospital bed, feeding him and stroking his little feet. In between he gazed at me and snoozed, snuffling and wriggling. I even managed to get a little sleep.

Visiting started at ten, just before the doctor came around to check on me. Everything had gone so smoothly; there were no reasons for me to stay. As soon as Neil arrived, I could go home.

When the door opened a tiny bit I thought it was him at first, but the cherubic Ruby appeared with a big grin on her face.

"Nicola." Ruby yelled, and ran to the bed, her blue eyes wide at the sight of the baby. Rebecca and Elliot followed behind.

"Hey, sweet pea. Want to see Noah?"

She nodded, her plaits flying, and Elliot lifted her onto the bed beside me.

"He's so little," Ruby said.

"Let me see. He's your ..." I hadn't thought about this before, and I laughed as I realised just how this little guy was related to her, "uncle."

Ruby giggled. "Uncle Noah?"

"I'm pretty sure you can just call him Noah. Isn't he precious?"

She nodded. Her hands were straight down by her sides, and she sat stiff as a board.

"Do you want to touch him? I bet he'd love a kiss."

"He's tiny," she whispered.

"You won't hurt him. I'm right here."

She leaned over, pursing her lips and kissing him on the cheek just as he sneezed. Ruby sprung back as she giggled. "Ewww."

"Now you're all covered in baby snot." I laughed.

"You're looking good." Rebecca stood beside the bed, rubbing my arm and leaning over to kiss me on the cheek.

"Thank you. I'm tired. It took quite an effort to get this one to join us. But he's here now."

"Did you manage to get any sleep?"

"A little. I think I'm still running on adrenalin. I'll be home later today. You guys are just so quick getting up here for a visit."

Ruby grinned, leaning in to take another look at the baby. He gazed at her with his big blue eyes.

"Ruby was so anxious to see Noah. I think it's because she's mega excited about becoming a big sister," Rebecca said.

I laughed. "I don't blame you, Ruby. I bet being a big sister will be so awesome."

Rebecca made grabby hands toward Noah. "Speaking of being a big sister, let me have a cuddle with my little brother."

Letting out another laugh, I gently passed her the baby. She rocked him in her arms and Elliot moved behind her, watching over her shoulder.

"That'll be you two soon." I grinned at Elliot.

"I can't wait." He looked down at Noah. "You are pretty awesome, little baby."

The door creaked as it opened again, and Neil shook his head as he entered the room. "You three are here early."

"Poppa!" Ruby cried, reaching up for him as he approached the bed. She wrapped her arms around his neck as he strained to lean over and kiss me.

"Hey, baby girl. Have you seen Noah?"

Her eyes grew big. "He's so tiny." She held her hands up, centimetres apart to show how small the baby was.

"He's *that* small?" Neil's amusement was clear in his tone, but Ruby nodded.

"But he's gonna grow *real* big. Just like Becca's baby."

"Not too big or Becca will have trouble getting the baby out." Rebecca laughed. She jiggled Noah. "You're so beautiful, widdle baby, you are." I'd never heard such a tone from her, and I caught Elliot's gaze, shaking my head as I watched my friend with my child.

His guffaw woke Rebecca out of her trance. "What?"

"Are you going to do the baby talk with our baby?"

She shrugged, and reached up to tickle his chin. "Maybe. Would Elliot like me to do it for him?"

"I think you already did. You're pregnant enough." She rolled her eyes as I teased her.

As she sat in the chair beside the bed, Elliot hovering over her, I leaned over to rest my head on Neil's arm and sighed.

"Tired?" he asked, kissing me on the temple.

"We didn't do too badly. I'll be glad to get back into my own bed. We can go home at any time."

"I think we need to give them a moment." He nodded toward Rebecca and Elliot. Ruby wriggled a bit closer, and I pulled her into my arms.

The previous night I'd looked around at Neil and Noah and considered the three of us my family. Now I saw the bigger reality. This was my family.

"Did you know, I think that Noah and Rebecca's baby is going to be very lucky?" I whispered to Ruby.

She leaned back, cupping my face in her hands.

"Do you want to know why?"

Ruby nodded, her expression so serious it made me smile.

"Because they'll have you. You'll be the best big sister and friend that he or she could ask for."

I reached up, pushing a stray hair off her face. "You come and see Noah whenever you want to."

She nodded, still so solemn. Ruby would take on her new role with vigour. I couldn't wait to see her and the other children play.

So much to look forward to.

TWENTY-ONE

I LOVED HIM.

Neil lay on our bed, watching over our two-month-old sleeping baby with so much adoration in his eyes. We would never go the same way he and Erica did. I'd love this man for the rest of my life, as he'd love me.

"Need anything?" I asked.

He looked up, shaking his head. "I'm fine, thanks. What are you doing for the rest of the day?"

"I thought I might quit my job."

He grinned. "Why the change of heart?"

"Because I can be at home with Noah and do what I want. It might be a juggle sometimes, but Rebecca will take some time off work soon and I can hang out with her. Plus, I've got an email from a former client asking if I'm still working for Renee."

His grin grew wider. "Well, that's good. I'm going to assume you'll be taking up my offer."

I shrugged. "Maybe."

"You have your design space. We can turn that small bedroom by the living room into an office. I'll hire someone to redecorate it. Know any good designers?"

Rolling my eyes and shaking my head, I turned back toward the bedroom door. "I'll see you soon."

Glancing over my shoulder, I watched as Neil leaned over Noah. "Your mother's going to go and slay a big, bad dragon. I wish I could be a fly on the wall to see that."

I laughed all the way to my car.

THE ELEVATOR SHUDDERED ALL the way up, and I smiled at the knowledge that this would be the last time I'd have to endure its rickety ways.

My stomach flipped as I approached the office, and I took a deep breath as I opened the outer door.

"Nicola." Cherie grinned as I entered. "Where's the baby?"

"At home with Neil. I came in to sort some things out."

"Renee's in her office. Just go through. Tamara will be over the moon to see you." She frowned. "She's been working extra hard."

"Well, if Renee knew how to do the job herself, she wouldn't notice me not being here so much."

I left Cherie gaping at the reception desk as I walked through to the offices.

"Nicola." Tamara jumped out of her seat, rushing at me. "Where's the baby?"

I laughed. "I'm beginning to think he's more popular than I am. He's at home with Neil. I just have to sort out a few things."

"Are you coming back to work soon? Cherie and I have missed you soooo much."

I licked my lips, taking a deep breath. "About that."

Her jaw dropped. "You're not coming back?" she whispered the words.

Renee's office door flew open. "Tamara, can I get the Timmins design? I'm beginning to think you've picked up Nicola's bad habit of being late with everything." Her head was bowed as she stared at her tablet screen.

"Nicola was usually late because Nicola was helping Tamara. Tamara needs help and support, not to be dumped in the deep end." I didn't know where the words came from, but satisfaction poured from me as Renee looked up with a glare in her eyes.

"Nicola," she hissed. "To what do we owe the pleasure of your company?" Her tone was bitter, and I couldn't be happier for the news I was about to deliver.

"I just came in to tell you I won't be coming back to work."

Tamara laughed, clapping her hand over her mouth.

Renee shot her a glare. "I see. I had hoped you would want to retain your independence after having the baby. Not let yourself and your talent get lost in a sea of nappies."

Oh, what a forked tongue.

"It won't. I'll take a break for a while, spend time with Noah while he's small. Enough time for my restraint of trade clause to lapse. Then I'll be going into business for myself." I grinned, fist-pumping. "Watch out world."

A look of such displeasure swept Renee's face that somewhere deep inside I longed to throw a bucket of water over her, just to see if she would melt.

"I see. It must be nice to have someone who can pay for everything."

"Working from home will reduce my overheads considerably. I'm just lucky I have a partner who supports and encourages me."

I held my head high. Nothing she said could bring me down. I had everything. My wonderful, amazing Neil who adored me, our beautiful baby, and a loving family. I'd never felt so fulfilled. The urge to draw would never leave me and now I could nurture it, break out from the shell I'd hidden in for so long, show the world what I was capable of.

Reaching into my bag, I pulled out my resignation letter. "So, if you could please arrange for any and all final pay to be put into my account as soon as possible, I would appreciate it."

"Clear out your desk and I'll sort this." Her tone was icy. I guessed she realised there was no point in making things harder.

"There's not a lot to clear. I'll just be a few minutes."

She turned on her heel, stalking back into her office and slamming the door.

Tamara grinned. "Good for you."

"The only concern I have is you. What are you going to do?"

She leaned over her desk. "I've got another job to go to," she whispered.

"You're kidding me." I dropped my voice. "Congratulations."

Tamara nodded toward Renee's office. "She's going to have a fit, but I don't care. She's been even more difficult since you've been on maternity leave."

This was it. Renee would never cope with both of us gone. Hopefully the next people she employed would make her pay properly for their talents.

I grabbed my mug from my desk. It was about the only thing that I had sitting on it that wasn't work-related.

"That's me. I'm out of here."

Tamara rushed from behind her desk and wrapped her arms around me. "I am going to miss you so much."

"We can stay in touch. Besides, maybe one day you can come and work for me. If you're not already in business for yourself."

She squeezed me tight. "Give that beautiful baby of yours a big kiss for me. And that man of yours."

"I will," I whispered, taking a deep breath to hold back the tears. Tamara and Cherie would be all I missed of this job.

Cherie hugged me as I reached reception. "This place won't be the same without you."

I shrugged. "I'll miss you too."

As I entered the rickety old elevator for the final time, I took one last look back at the offices of Jameson Interiors. The designer before me had gone onto bigger and better things.

Would Renee be so lucky finding talent the third time around?

I reached the car, unlocking the door and sinking into the driver's seat. Leaning back, I closed my eyes. As satisfying as that was, it would be weird not to go back. Neil had turned my life around, and I adored him for it. Now I could start again and really make a name for myself, not be hidden behind someone else.

Slotting the key in the ignition I turned it. The car shuddered, reluctant to come to life. The poor thing needed a service again, but my final pay should cover that.

I patted the dashboard. "Come on, old girl. Let's get home to Neil and Noah."

Just saying their names filled me with the warmth that love gave.

I loved going home.

NEIL WAS asleep when I got back. He'd moved Noah to his crib and my boy was also asleep. He'd been up a few times in the night, so we were all tired. Hopefully they both got the rest they needed.

After quitting my job, I was way too excited to rest. I retrieved some chicken drumsticks from the freezer, rolling them in egg and breadcrumbs before placing them in the oven to cook. I threw together some lettuce leaves and various other salad ingredients, stirring them around as I lost myself in thought over the afternoon's events.

Neil's lips grazed my neck and I laughed, leaning back against him.

"The deed is done?" he murmured in my ear.

"The witch is dead." I laughed. "Tamara has a new job, too. Renee won't be happy to find that one out."

He nuzzled my ear. "Serves her right. If she provided a supportive working environment, it wouldn't be an issue."

I sighed, closing my eyes.

"How long until dinner?"

"A little while. I just put the chicken in the oven."

He spun me around. "How about we sneak off for some us time before Noah wakes up? I could do with paying you a little attention."

"I could do with having that attention. Feels like forever."

His eyes softened as he scanned my features. "I love you, Nicola."

"I love you, too. And I love your idea. I think we've got about twenty minutes before the chicken is cooked."

Neil licked his lips, waggling his eyebrows. "I can work with twenty minutes."

"Noah could wake before then too."

"I can work with ten."

TWENTY-TWO

WATCHING Neil with Rebecca's baby was almost as enjoyable as seeing him with our son. The birth of Anna gave him so much joy, and I loved him more than ever.

When I'd met him, he'd been so focused on his business. He still was, but he'd eased back on the control, preferring to spend quality time with his family. Having Ruby join the family brought him so much pleasure. That little girl had been through so much for her age, and now Rebecca and Elliot gave her the stability she needed. Neil revelled in her calling him Poppa.

Anna was a lot like Rebecca, and I think Neil saw himself in there, too. The children enhanced his relationship with his daughter, which made me happy. Rebecca and I had become closer friends than ever.

And then there was Noah. Rebecca hadn't seen a lot of her father when she was growing up, but Neil was determined not to let that be the case for our little boy. He was so hands on, changing nappies, rocking him to sleep—our little family was perfect.

Noah was six months old now, a smiling happy boy who was the best piece of artwork I could ever have hoped to produce. We'd spent the day inside, the rain pouring as the weather grew colder. Soon came winter, and we snuggled up on the couch watching our baby try desperately to crawl. These were the best days.

"It won't be long now," Neil murmured in my ear as Noah rocked back and forward on the rug.

"He'll be all over the place."

"Happy?" He nuzzled my neck.

"More than ever."

"I didn't think it was possible to be this happy." My heart fluttered as he said the words. We'd done so much for each other just by falling in love. "Would you still love me if I had nothing?"

My heart sunk. "Why would you ask that?"

He clamped his lips together and said nothing as he cast his eyes across his face.

"Neil? If we had nothing we'd still be together. It's not like I haven't been there before. Are you okay?"

He nodded. "There's a deal at work that's gone sour. It's not huge, but it's bigger than the deal that sunk my relationship with Erica. None of this is at risk, but I just needed to know."

I smiled at him affectionately, cupping his face and kissing him on the nose. "I love the life we have, but if we lost it all we'd have each other. I would never walk away from you, no matter what. Hell, worse-case scenario, we can pitch a tent in a paddock at my parents and eat the free-range eggs my mother sells."

"Have I told you lately just how much I love you?" Neil's smile spread across his face, and he shook his head.

"I only ever wanted you for you. Although, I have to admit your car is pretty nice. We could always try and live in that."

He laughed as he pursed his lips to kiss me, and I sighed at the feel of his arms around my waist. I could sit here forever with him like this, content and knowing I was loved for me and only me. There were no strings attached to any part of our relationship. This was unconditional and forever.

Nothing would ever come between us.

Neil pecked me on the lips. "I'll go and check on dinner. I bet Noah's hungry after all that effort."

I switched my gaze back to Noah as he rocked and managed to move forward about an inch.

"Go, baby!" I called.

Noah grinned as he looked up at me. He was pleased with himself, and that crooked smile he gave with the two teeth he'd cut made me grin in return.

"Nicola?" Neil paused in the doorway, the colour draining from his face as I watched. The happy smile on his face disappeared in an instant.

"Neil?"

"I just need to catch my breath."

His skin seemed suddenly so pale, and he gulped for air as he made his way back to the couch.

Panic gripped my throat, but I had to control it. Neil needed help.

"Tell me what's going on."

"My chest hurts. There's a pain running down my arm."

Shit. I'd seen my father go through this.

"I'm going to call an ambulance," I said.

"I'll be fine. Just give me a minute." He gave me a faint smile.

"No such luck. I've seen this before." I ran to the kitchen and grabbed the phone off the wall. The three rings that it took emergency services to answer seemed like an eternity as I watched Neil in the next room. He sat, his face etched in discomfort, his right hand rubbing his left arm.

"Ambulance, please. I think my partner is having a heart attack." The woman took my details as I kept an eye on Neil, the pain etched on his face.

We lived not far from the hospital, and I put down the phone once I knew they were coming.

"They're on their way. Won't be too long."

"Stop fussing, Nicola." He smiled, but it was strained.

I scooped Noah up in my arms and sat back on the couch beside Neil while we waited. The ten minutes it took for the ambulance felt like hours until the knock finally came at the door.

The paramedics sat either side of Neil, testing his oxygen levels.

"Nicola? Are you okay?" he asked as they took his readings.

"I'll be fine when I know you will be." That was the only answer I could give.

"We need to get him in to the hospital. Did you want to

ride in the ambulance with us?" The paramedic smiled reassuringly.

"Um, I need to bring my baby. It might be better if I drive for myself."

"Are you going to be alright to do that?" Neil's voice made me roll my eyes. Here he was having some kind of turn, and all he cared about was me.

"I'll have to be. I'll call Rebecca too."

"Thank you," he said quietly.

I leaned over and kissed him on the forehead. "I love you."

"I love you too."

"We have to get him going." The paramedic sounded apologetic, and I nodded. "We'll take him to Accident and Emergency first."

"I'll be right behind you," I said.

"Take my car," Neil called as they carried him out the door.

If I did take his car, I could call Rebecca on Bluetooth. Neil had bought me a new phone not long ago, and I was relieved to have it. At least I could make calls on the move now without worrying about it.

While all this had gone on, Noah had fallen asleep in my arms. Transferring him to one side, I grabbed his nappy bag and my handbag with my other hand and dumped them on the kitchen bench, turning off the oven and the elements.

He stirred, and I stroked his little hands. "Let's go see, Daddy," I whispered.

Neil's car was parked in the garage, and I threw my bags

in the back seat, buckling in my baby. He protested but didn't open his eyes, settling instead.

My hands shook as I sat in the driver's seat and held the steering wheel. It wasn't a long drive, but my trembling wasn't going to help me. I had to get this under control.

I pressed the buttons to dial Rebecca, and her cheerful voice filled the car. "Hey, Nicola. What's up?"

"Your dad has just gone to hospital. I think he's had a heart attack." My voice wobbled as I said the words, but I had to get this over with before going out onto the road.

"Shit." Her voice broke. "I'll head there now."

"They said they'll go to A and E first. Meet you there?"

She let out a breath. At least she would have Elliot there to take care of her. "We'll sort the kids out and get there as quickly as possible."

I closed my eyes as tears rolled down my cheeks. Not that I'd had any doubt she'd come, but knowing Rebecca would be at the hospital helped.

"Are you okay?" she asked.

"I will be when I know he's alright."

"See you soon."

I hung up the phone and started the car. Noah stirred in the back seat. "Hang in there, sweet pea. We'll be at the hospital shortly."

As I drove the short distance, a million thoughts went through my head. With Neil being that much older than me, there would more than likely come a time when I would end up letting him go. I didn't want to think about it, but how could I not? As strong and capable as he was, he was also human, but we hadn't had enough time together.

I turned into the hospital car park and found a park a short walk from the entrance. Scooping Noah out of his car seat, I weaved my way between cars and in the front doors of the Accident and Emergency department.

Neil was having tests done, and I had never felt so helpless in all my life. With nothing else to do, I sat in the waiting room rocking Noah, tears streaming down my cheeks. After everything, this couldn't be it. Could it? My chest was about to burst with the pain inside.

"Nicola?" Rebecca sat beside me, Elliot taking Noah from me so Rebecca could wrap her arms around my shoulders.

"Where are the kids?" I didn't even know why that was my first thought.

"With Olivia and Logan. Their house is chaotic as it is—another two children won't make much difference."

I laughed despite myself, sniffing and wiping my eyes.

"Have you heard anything?"

I shook my head. "Nothing since I arrived. He was this awful shade of grey, and all he cared about was how I was coping."

She rolled her eyes, rubbing my back. "That's Dad for you. We'll keep you company for however long it takes."

"Thanks." I rested my head against her while she hugged me tight.

"He'll be okay. I'm sure of it. My dad is bulletproof," she whispered.

"I hope so. I'm so scared, Rebecca."

"So am I. Let's just sit here for a while like this."

I sighed. "That's fine with me."

The hospital was quiet, but for the occasional gurgle from

Noah. Elliot tickled him under the chin, keeping him occu-pied while we waited.

"What do you think, Becs? Should we try for a boy?" Elliot's expression was hopeful.

She laughed. "Only if you can push him out your vagina."

He gave her that 'you'll keep' look, and shook his head. I smiled at their closeness. For so long it had seemed like none of us would find that special someone, yet all of us had managed to do it around the same time. Elliot and Rebecca had recently become engaged, and Neil and I had been so happy for them. At least if this was it, he'd seen his daughter settle down.

Stop it.

"Nicola Crandell?"

I looked up. An older man in blue scrubs approached, maybe the same age as Neil. Rebecca's nails dug into my arm and we stood together in a unified front.

"Yes?"

"I'm Doctor Lawrence. I need to speak to you about Neil Wallace."

I nodded. "This is his daughter, Rebecca. Please. Tell us what's going on."

To my complete and utter relief, he smiled. It wasn't a big smile, but it was something. "Neil has had a coronary episode, or what you might call a heart attack."

I gripped Rebecca tightly. "Is he going to be okay?"

"It was reasonably mild, but he needs to be here for some tests and for us to keep an eye on him. In plain English, he has a clogged artery, so we will have to perform an angioplasty."

"What's that?"

"He'll have an angiogram tomorrow. We'll run some dye to find out where the blockage is and then we'll book him in to clear it out. We're just moving him up to the cardiac ward where we'll keep an eye on him."

I nodded again, trying to take it all in.

"What caused it? He's so healthy. He keeps fit, and he has regular check-ups." Rebecca spoke up now.

"His cholesterol is quite high. Not overly, but enough to help cause an issue. His blood pressure was right up."

"I think he's been under quite a lot of stress lately," I said quietly.

Rebecca's eyebrows shot up. "He has?"

"Some work stuff. I'll tell you about it later."

She frowned. "I want to know the details." She shifted her gaze to the doctor. "When can we see him?"

He nodded. "Ms Crandell, if you want to come with me."

"But Rebecca ..." I started.

"We need to give Neil some space. He's been through a lot." The doctor smiled sympathetically. It didn't make me feel any better.

Rebecca nudged me. "Go up to the ward. I'll wait to see him."

"Are you sure?"

She shrugged. "Dad needs to be better. Crowding him is the last thing he needs."

"Thank you." I hugged her.

We walked through the hospital. I hadn't been here since giving birth to Noah, and I couldn't wait to leave. That feeling hung over me as I walked down the corridors. Neil needed to be home with me.

"Here we go." The doctor pointed at the door. He nodded toward some seats in the hallway. "Sorry it's not more comfortable, but if you'd like to wait here," he said to Rebecca.

"Won't be long." I rubbed Rebecca's arm as I said it. She would hate the thought of her father being in here as much as I did.

Tension crept through my shoulders at the sight of Neil. Cords ran to machines monitoring everything, the steady beep of the heart rate monitor bringing me some kind of strange comfort.

He smiled as I entered the room, taking my hand in his as I sat.

"You gave me such a fright," I whispered, kissing him on the temple.

"Sorry. I gave myself a fright."

He raised his palm to my cheek as tears rolled down my cheeks. "Nicola, it's okay. I'll be fine."

"I can't bear the thought of losing you."

"It'll happen one day. Maybe not today, but eventually. So there's something we need to talk about before that day comes."

I turned my head to kiss his palm. "What's that?"

"You. Me. Getting married."

Despite myself I laughed, a small bubble of snot growing from my nose. I shook my head, wiping my nose with my sleeve.

"That's classy, Miss Crandell."

"That's why you love me."

"Always." His voice was so croaky, not the usual smooth,

romantic tone he had, even if the words were perfect. "That's why when I get out of here, we are getting married. If you'll say yes."

"I'd marry you in a heartbeat."

"That might be all I have."

I closed my eyes and leaned over, resting my head on the cool, white bed sheet. "Don't say anything like that," I whispered.

"Whatever happens, you and Noah will be well taken care of. I want you to know that."

I sat back up. "I love you. You had better not leave me."

"I have no intention of leaving you. I just wanted you to know." He smiled. "I love you too. More than anything."

"Rebecca's outside. She wants to see you too. The doctor showed me through first." I placed my hand on his arm. For someone so strong, he seemed so frail right now. Despite the doctor's reassurance, seeing him like this scared the hell out of me.

"I need to see her too." He took a deep breath. "At least this means I get to slow down, spend some more time with you and Noah. Maybe it's time for me to retire." His lips quirked. "I'll be a house husband while you get your business going and provide for our family."

"Are you ready for that?"

"I would rather spend the rest of my days with you than running around chasing deals."

"I'm ready if you are." leaned over to kiss him again, lingering on his forehead. "I think I'd better let Rebecca have a turn now before she kicks the door in."

Neil gave me a faint smile. "I'd like to see her. Come back in a little while?"

"Of course."

At the door I paused, turning to take another look at him. His eyes were closed, and he looked peaceful at least. No more pain for the meantime. The thought of losing him made my own chest ache. Not after everything.

Rebecca waited outside, her hands clasped together as she kept her eyes on the door.

"Go in and see him."

She bolted before I had a chance to say anything else. Out of the corner of my eye, I caught Noah kicking and waving excitedly at the sight of me, and Elliot handed him over with a smile. I hugged him tight, breathing in that sweet baby smell.

"Daddy's okay, baby. He's just gotta stay here for a while."

Elliot gripped my shoulder. "Anything you need, Nicola. We're here."

I smiled. "I think we all just need to stick together. Getting him to relax is going to be the tricky part."

"We'll help you work on that. You're far from alone."

TWENTY-THREE

I'D SAT with Neil again for a while after Rebecca had seen him. The medication and the effort to do anything had tired him, and he soon fell asleep still holding my hand.

"I'll be back in the morning," I whispered, kissing him on the forehead. I lingered, letting go of his hand. He was where he needed to be, but that didn't make me any less scared.

Rebecca sat outside with Noah and slipped her arm around my shoulders as I sat beside her.

"He's asleep and comfortable," I whispered.

"Let's get you home and get Noah into bed. Elliot's gone to get Ruby and Anna. We'll stay with you tonight if that works for you."

I nodded. "I'd appreciate that."

"Truth be told, I think I need that as much as you do." Her voice shook as she spoke, and I leaned in against her.

"We'll get through this. We have to."

She carried my bags as we walked back out of the hospital

and toward the car park. This had to be the hardest part—leaving Neil here while I went home. Despite him being asleep and needing the doctors to take care of him now, a huge part of me wanted to take him back to our place. Since I'd moved in with him, we'd spent one night apart, when Noah was born.

My bed would be cold and lonely tonight.

"I'll drive," Rebecca said.

Any other time I might have fought her for it since I loved that car so much, but tonight I was content to ride in the back seat with Noah and close my eyes. With all the worry, sitting in the hospital was tiring. It'd be so good to be home again.

Elliot had parked outside when we got there, and greeted us in the garage as we drove in.

"Ruby's asleep and tucked into bed. Anna is on the living room floor and grizzling. I think she's hungry." He kissed Rebecca tenderly as she walked into the house.

"How are you holding up?" he asked. I unbuckled Noah and lifted him out of his seat.

"I'm okay, I think. It's still sinking in."

"I saw that your dinner was half-cooked. I cleaned it all up and dug some steak out of the freezer. Figured you and Becs would be hungry."

Patting him on the chest as I walked past, I nodded. "I didn't realise how hungry until you mentioned it."

"I cut up some potatoes to make fries and I'll just throw the steaks on now. Gotta keep you fed."

As I stepped inside the house, I turned. "Thanks, Elliot. You're a good man."

Rebecca had already made it to the couch and Anna was

feeding hungrily. Noah had fed at the hospital, and I didn't bother changing him into his pyjamas. He might wake in the night with this disrupted evening, but for the moment he was asleep.

I dropped my bags and headed up the hallway. Noah went down in his cot with barely a whimper, and by the time I got back to the living room the scent of frying potatoes and meat made my mouth water.

"Elliot grabbed the portable cot from home, so we're good." Rebecca rocked Anna and I sat beside them, smiling at that sated milk-hangover look on Anna's face.

"She's such a sweet baby," I said.

"She is the best. Apart from Noah. We have such amazing kids."

I laughed. "Whoever thought we'd be so settled."

Rebecca stood and carried Anna from the room. My stomach grumbled from the scent of Elliot's cooking, and I walked to the kitchen to investigate.

"That smells amazing."

He looked up from the frying pan. "I hope it's as good as it smells."

"Rebecca's told me about what a good cook you are."

Elliot smiled. "I wish this dinner was under better circumstances."

I fought tears and my lips refused to turn up.

"Nicola, he'll be okay. He's got too much going for him to give up."

"I know, I just hate him going through this," I whispered.

Elliot turned and wrapped me up in a bear hug. "You and Noah are what he has to live for. I keep thinking about what

Becs and Anna and Ruby mean to me, and I can't breathe at the thought of anything happening to any of them. And I'd sure as shit fight to stay by their sides. He'll do the same for you."

I nodded, closing my eyes and just let Elliot support me. He was right, and I knew it. I was tired and scared and just needed Neil to be well again.

"Nicola?" Rebecca came up behind me, and Elliot let go so she could envelop me in her arms. "Love you," she whispered.

"Love you too. All of you. I don't know what I'd do without you."

"You're stuck with us now," she said, and I raised my head to look at her. "I mean, I could always ditch you as a friend, not so easy when you're my step-mother."

I laughed, and wiped the tears from my eyes. "Stop with the step-mother thing."

"I can't while it still gets that reaction." She laughed.

"If you ladies want to take a seat at the table, I'll serve up dinner," Elliot spoke up, and Rebecca let me go.

"You heard the man. Let's sit down. I'm starving."

I sat at the table and watched as Elliot placed my plate in front of me, and then served Rebecca. What I would have done without them, I didn't know.

I'd be eternally grateful for their presence as we all brought comfort to each other.

SLEEP WAS hard to come by after all the months I'd lain beside Neil. His scent graced the pillow and sheets, and I closed my eyes and tried so hard to embrace elusive dreams of better times.

Noah woke a little after four, wanting his middle-of-the-night feed and Mummy time. Our usual routine was to sit in the living room rather than disrupt Neil, who would get up early to go to work. This time, I took Noah back to bed with me, and once he'd drunk his fill and had his nappy changed, he fell asleep beside me, snuggled in my arms. After that he slept the rest of the night, and I slept better with him next to me. It wasn't the same as having Neil there, but Noah's presence brought the comfort I craved.

When I woke, the bedside clock said 9.02 a.m. and Noah still slept peacefully beside me. The ward would open up at ten.

I lifted the baby gently and took him to his room, placing him in his cot. He'd be awake soon enough. There was no point getting him up too early.

The scent of bacon filled the house, and I smiled at the kitchen door. Elliot stood over the frying pan, the sizzle of food prompting my stomach to grumble.

"How are you doing this morning?" Rebecca asked as I sat at the table.

"Tired. I didn't sleep to start with. Noah slept so well too. I didn't leave him in his cot; I took him back to bed with me. I think that's what helped in the end."

She nodded. "Want some breakfast? Elliot's making bacon sandwiches."

I grimaced. "I think I'll stick with coffee."

"Are you sure? I wasn't a huge fan until they became our thing."

"Live a little, Nicola. There was plenty of bacon in the fridge," Elliot said. I laughed, rolling my eyes at him. I could see why Rebecca liked him so much—he had this gentle way about him, adored the hell out of her, and had the most amazing dimples.

"I know. I bought it. Go on, then. Get me a bacon sandwich."

Rebecca stood, grabbing a tea towel from where it sat on the counter. Scrunching one end up in her hand, she flicked it across Elliot's backside.

"You heard the lady. Get to work." She laughed.

"See what I have to put up with?" He grinned. They were so good together.

"You poor thing," I said.

Rebecca moved to stand beside Elliot, pouring me a coffee before I'd gotten up the motivation to stand. "Here you go. And ignore him. He loves it."

"Thanks. I need to eat this and get to the hospital."

She rested her hand on mine as she sat back beside me. "I called earlier. He's still stable."

I placed my hand over hers. "Thank you. I have to admit it was weird not having him beside me last night. Guess I have to get used to that for a while."

Rebecca nodded, giving Elliot a sly smile as he placed a plate with a bacon sandwich on it in front of me.

"How was your night?" I asked.

"We did it in my old bed. That's one for the bucket list," she said, waggling her eyebrows.

"I thought we had a no-sharing policy."

"That's just for you and my dad having sex. Nothing else is off-limits."

"It is if I have to change the sheets." I laughed. It was so good having her here. I couldn't wait for Neil to come home, but in the meantime, Rebecca's company was soothing.

"I can sort that out. Just point me in the direction of the linen cupboard." Elliot carried three more plates to the table, setting them down. "Ruby, breakfast is ready."

She came running in from the living room, and stood between Rebecca and I. "Where?"

"Over here." Her father pointed at the chair opposite me. Ruby ran the short distance and jumped up.

"Good morning, Ruby," I said.

"Good morning," she mumbled, having taken a big mouthful of food.

"Anna not awake yet?"

Rebecca sighed. "She woke a couple of times in the night. I just got her back to sleep. We'll come to the hospital, but it might be a little later."

I picked up my sandwich and took a bite. After a rough start to the night, this hit the spot. Elliot's obsession with bacon sandwiches made sense all of a sudden. This had to be the perfect start to the day.

"That's how I reacted when I tried it the first time." Rebecca nudged my elbow.

"What?"

"That moaning sound you just made."

"I didn't make a moaning sound."

Rebecca rolled her eyes, giving me a knowing grin. "Sure you did. I heard it. It wasn't very loud, but it was there."

"Daddy's sandwiches are awesome," Ruby mumbled again before swallowing down the last of her food.

How could I go wrong when I had such a wonderful family surrounding me? No matter what choices we made, whether Neil went back to work or did as he'd suggested and retired, we had the greatest supporters under our roof right now.

We'd fight back from this, get his health back on track, and get his business sorted out.

Together.

TWENTY-FOUR

Rebecca's father took me by the hand, and together we walked to the front of our small congregation in the registry office.

All the people we loved were with us—my parents, Rebecca and Elliot, Ruby, Anna, and Noah. Our extended family were there, too. Katya, Tim, and their baby girl, Portia, Gemma and Justin. Tamara and Cherie.

When I once had friends and yet felt so alone, now I had all these wonderful people around me who loved us as much as we loved them.

Before them all, I swore to love Neil until the end of my days. I meant it. He was mine, the right person for me, the one who I had grown with over this past year. He loved me for me, and nothing and no one would ever come between us.

Not to mention that when he got to kiss the bride, it was the hottest thing in my entire life.

Then we went home for a party.

Elliot cooked bacon. It was still their family staple, and I had to admit I was quite partial to it too. Neil had been so good with his diet since the heart attack, and we had both worked a little harder at keeping fit and being healthy. If not for our own sakes, then for the sake of our children. My husband was in pretty good shape for a man approaching sixty.

The memory of the time in hospital still haunted me, and if anything I was more cautious about everything than he was.

We sat in the corner of the living room, feeding each other wedding cake and snuggling.

"Today's been perfect," Neil murmured in my ear, planting a kiss just below it.

"Better than perfect." I tilted my head toward him, nuzzling his nose.

"I didn't know if we'd ever make it this far."

I raised my hand to stroke his cheek. "Well, here we are."

His eyes flashed with desire. "Here we are." He looked around the room. The kids were outside with Katya, Tim and Gemma. Rebecca and Elliot hung around the kitchen. Noah had already been napping for half an hour. "Want to sneak off?"

"On our wedding day?"

Neil shrugged. "We have a reputation to uphold."

I laughed. "Let's not get caught this time."

"Is that a yes?"

The intensity with which he looked at me made me catch my breath. Whatever happened in the future, here and now, I was all he wanted. He was all I needed.

"We need to make it quick." I wanted him. Right there and right then.

"Where do you suggest?"

I grabbed his hand and stood, pulling him to his feet. Another quick look around and I set off toward the hallway with him in tow. When we got to our bedroom door, I pulled him inside, laughing as he wrapped his arms around me. Behind him the door closed, and he claimed my lips with his own, kissing me deeply and leaving me breathless.

"You're so naughty, Mrs Wallace." He dropped his head to my neck, taking nips with his teeth of my skin. I moaned, pressing myself against him, triggering some distant memory of our first kiss, the first time my body and his were together.

"Hmmm. Mrs Wallace," I said, laughing softly as I turned around and bent over the bed, lifting the hem of my knee length white dress until it was over my waist. I slipped my panties down my legs and left them dangling on one ankle as Neil ran his hands down my back, sighing as he touched my bare skin.

"You are breathtaking," he said.

"Are you talking about from that particular angle or just in general?" I teased. He ran his hands between my legs and behind me came the sound of him unzipping his pants.

"You. All of you. I love you more than I could ever put into words."

Freaking typical. My eyes welled with tears as he pushed into me, and I straightened up a little as he pulled me back against him.

"Stop making me cry while we're having sex."

Neil ran a finger down my cheek and brushed his lips up

my neck as he moved inside me. "As long as you're crying because you're happy and not because you're sad," he whispered.

He moved his hand back down again, working his magic with his fingers, leaving me sighing into his mouth. His tongue lashed against mine as our kiss deepened and he let out a groan, gripping my thighs tight enough that there had to be marks.

"Oh, give me a break." Rebecca's voice came from the door, and I chuckled as the click told me she'd closed it again.

Neil planted a kiss on my earlobe, shaking with laughter as he pulled out of me.

"It had to be her," I said.

"Serves her right for walking into a room where the door was closed." Neil zipped up, pecking me on the lips as I turned around.

"I'll be out in a moment. Just need to sort myself out," I said. My heart, so full of affection for this man, seemed to grow as we gazed at one another.

"Don't take too long." He pulled me into his arms and ran his hands down my back.

Noah's scream broke the quiet. The whole world had to know when he was awake.

"I'll go get our son. See you in the living room in a minute."

"Okay." I pressed my lips to his, reaching for his hands and squeezing them. Our life together just got better by the day. My business was growing fast, as was our child. Every day we got to spend time together and every night was filled with more love than I'd ever thought possible.

He grinned and made his way out of the room. Noah would yell again soon if he didn't get some attention, but Daddy would be able to distract him for a few minutes.

I sighed, and walked to our en suite to freshen up before heading out to the living room.

Sure enough, Neil sat on the couch, rocking our son on his knee. Noah's eyes were rimmed red, and he grumped and grizzled until I took him and raised him to my breast.

"He so cranky. I think that's just what he needed," he crooned, stroking his head.

Once he'd had a drink he'd be more awake and happy, and we'd be back to our peaceful day.

"I'm going to go and see how Ruby and Anna are doing." Neil pecked me on the cheek.

I closed my eyes, rocking Noah as he kept drinking. The sofa sank, and I smiled at Rebecca as she sat. "Hey."

"You and Dad. Still can't keep your hands of each other." She rolled her eyes.

"It is our wedding day. You should have knocked," I teased.

"I did. I thought Dad was outside with the kids and it was just you in there. No wonder you didn't hear me, being *that* distracted."

I leaned back and sighed. "I love your dad so much."

Rebecca gave me such an affectionate look. "I know, and you know what? Maybe I wouldn't have picked you for Dad's partner a while ago, but you two work. You changed his life, and I'll always be grateful for that."

"He changed my life. He's so special. I love how it brought us closer too."

"I might give you crap about being my step-mother, but you're like a sister to me."

I nodded. "That's how I feel too."

Noah let go and wiggled off my lap. Anna and Ruby stood in the doorway, and Rebecca and I, leaning against each other, watched our children play together happily. Neil caught my gaze from across the room, and we shared a look that warmed me from my head to my toes.

"Where did Elliot go?" I asked.

"To get your wedding present." Rebecca waggled her eyebrows at me, and I narrowed my eyes in response.

"I thought we said no wedding presents."

"Not from us. From Dad to you." She grinned, and I screwed up my mouth as I continued to give her a dirty look.

Neil grabbed my hand. "Come outside. I've got something for you."

I stood, following him out to the driveway. His car sat out there, with a white ribbon on top of it, like a gift.

"What on earth are you doing? Why is your car dressed up?" I laughed.

"It's not my car."

Confused, I frowned. "What do you mean it's not your car?"

"I mean, I bought you one of your own. I've let you drive around in that death mobile for too long as it is. I know how much you love my car, so I got you one too."

My stomach fell to my knees at the thought of such luxury. For a man who had been so concerned not that long ago about how I would deal with living on nothing, this was such an extravagant gesture. I didn't think I'd had anything of my own so expensive in my entire life.

"So? What do you think?"

I threw my arms around his neck and covered him in kisses. "If we ever lost everything, we'd have two cars to live in?"

Neil roared with laughter. "Happy wedding day, Nicola."

"I love it. Thank you."

He kissed the top of my head as I snuggled in against him. I'd never been so spoiled in all my life. And love. So much love. My heart was whole, content with it all I wanted for nothing, materially and emotionally.

Still, if we lost all the money tomorrow, I'd still have the man who would love me forever, and our child.

Nothing could stop us now.

TWENTY-FIVE

ONE YEAR LATER …

"TAMARA, how are you doing on that project for Faraday Travel?" I asked as I walked into the living room. She sat in the middle of the floor, paper strewn everywhere. She still got easily flustered, but since she'd come to work for me the month before, she'd started to relax a little and her designs had been so much better than anything she'd ever done for Renee.

"Don't fall over in shock, but I'm nearly finished."

I laughed and shook my head. "There's still a week until deadline, you crazy lady."

"Trust me, if this was back when we were both working for Renee, I'd be chewing the end of my pencil and wondering what to do past the colour of the walls."

A giggle came from behind me, and I turned to see Noah stampeding toward us.

"Where have you been?" I grabbed him as he ran up to my side and hugged him tight.

"We were out in the backyard." Neil leaned over to peck me on the lips.

"Have you been playing with Daddy?" Noah nodded, his infectious grin lighting up the room. "Want some juice?" I put him back down with a sigh. If I thought I'd been big with him, the baby I was now carrying seemed twice the size. Although, that might have been because I was eight months pregnant and over it all.

"I can get it," Neil said.

"No, you and Noah sit down. I need a drink anyway." As pregnant as I was, I still fretted over Neil's health. Not that it seemed I needed to. Since his angioplasty, he'd bounced back to where he'd been before, and a healthier diet and less stress had helped keep him that way. "Tamara, do you want anything?"

"I'll help." She'd tidied up her papers and stood. "I need to move; I've got a cramp in my thigh."

"That's what you get for working hard." I laughed.

She limped toward me, chuckling as she leaned on my shoulder. "Working like this makes me want to work hard. At least I feel like I'm doing something for myself."

"That's how I feel. Wonder how Renee's doing."

Tamara shrugged. "Maybe she's disappeared up her own—"

"Tamara! Noah's right here."

She laughed. "Sorry. You know it's true. Stay here and I'll go get us some drinks. Rest up with your family. I don't want you going into labour today; I might need your help."

I shook my head, and Neil took my hand and led me to

the couch. "She's right. You need to be putting your feet up more."

Leaning back, I closed my eyes. "I'm so ready for this to be over."

"Go and have a nap. Everything will still be here when you're done."

Neil had settled into retirement a lot easier than I'd thought he would. His CFO, Lance, had stepped in. They'd been friends for years, and Lance was a little younger than Neil and knew the business inside and out. Rebecca had bought a small publishing business, deciding to utilise her studies in English Literature to follow her own dreams. Lance and Neil had absorbed her subsidiary, keeping on the staff rather than letting it all go.

We all got what we wanted.

Maybe there was a big age gap between us, but Neil's retirement and my working from home meant we could spend as much time together as possible as we raised our family.

Noah climbed onto the couch, pushing his way between us, and I wrapped my arm around him. "Want a nap with Mummy?"

He nodded, yawning as he tried to place his arms over me.

"Not long now and that bump will be gone and I'll be much easier to snuggle with." I stood and picked him up, sitting him on my hip and kissing him all over his face as he giggled.

"Want to join us?" I asked Neil.

He shook his head. "As tempting as it is, I have a feeling

I'll be kicked out of the bed by this one." He tickled Noah under the chin.

I squeezed Noah and nodded. "I think you're right there."

"See you when you wake up."

I picked up Noah, carrying him to the bedroom. We snuggled down under the covers, and I slipped my arm under his head, stroking his forehead with my other hand. He gave me a hazy smile, until his little eyes closed and I shut my own to join him.

I MISSED the ceremony for the interior design awards. For the first time in my career I'd been nominated. It took branching out on my own to accomplish that. Early on in my business, I'd taken on a small job for a boutique recruiting company. For the first time I'd set my own rules, played my own game, and I had been so proud to be nominated for the award for my work on it.

Instead, I crawled into bed with my husband and made the most of the last nights before we were joined by our second child. As with Noah, we didn't want to know what we were having. It would be a wonderful surprise, whatever it was. Despite my excitement about being nominated, getting a decent night's sleep beat anything and everything right now

I jumped as the phone rang. Since Noah, I hadn't been a heavy sleeper, and at a time when I had to orchestrate simply rolling over, it didn't take much to waken me.

I slapped the bedside cabinet until I laid my hand on it.

"Who's that?" Neil murmured beside me. He flicked on the bedside lamp and soft light filled the room.

"Tamara." I pushed a button. "Hello?"

"Holy-shit-Nicola-you-won."

I held up a hand. "Whoa. One word at a time. I didn't catch any of that. Are you okay? Do you need a taxi? An ambulance?" The bedside clock said it was still only 10.32 p.m.

"You won. You're the Emerging Designer of the Year. I accepted for you. They all laughed when I said you were worried your waters would break on stage."

Neil gripped my arm and I chuckled. I could just picture Tamara getting over-excited and telling the whole world our secrets. It didn't matter. It wasn't like I had anything to hide about my life anymore.

"What's going on?" Neil asked.

"I won the emerging designer award."

"Congrats, my clever, beautiful wife." He kissed my cheek and I leaned against him.

"Renee was there too. She managed to squeak out congratulations. She's selling her business. Moving on to other things, she said. I don't think she found anyone good enough to replace us."

For some reason it saddened me to hear that. Someone who could have had so much more, but screwed herself through short-sightedness. Tamara and I were so busy we were deferring work, turning it down if we had to. Our workloads were manageable, and we still had each other's backs.

"Anyway, I'm going to let you get back to sleep. I can hear it in your voice. Sweet dreams."

"Thanks for calling. We'll have to do something to celebrate."

"Maybe when you're not ready to drop. Talk to you tomorrow."

I hung up the phone, and Neil flung his arm over me. "I'm so proud of you."

I snuggled against him. "All this time and what I needed to do was go out on my own."

"Told you." He squeezed me tight before turning to his side and turning off the light.

Rolling over with a groan, I spooned as tight against him as I could, considering the big bump between us. "I couldn't have done it without you."

Neil snorted. "If you believe that, you're crazy."

I nuzzled the back of his neck. "Finding you gave me the freedom to be me."

He turned, and I just knew that if the light had been on, I'd have his blue gaze fixed on me. "You were already you." His hand landed softly on my face in the dark, and I closed my eyes as he stroked my cheek. "Our life together may have helped, but you found the strength to do all of this yourself. I'm just the man who was lucky enough to work out what an amazing woman you are. This is all yours."

I reached for his hand and kissed his palm.

He was my heart.

I loved my life.

ALSO BY WENDY SMITH

Coming Home

Doctor's Orders

Baker's Dozen

Hunter's Mark

Teacher's Pet

A Very Campbell Christmas

Fall and Rise Duet

Falling

Rising

Fall and Rise - The Complete Duet

The Aeon Series

Game On

Build a Nerd

Bar None

Hollywood Kiwis Series

Common Ground

Even Ground

Under Ground

Rocky Ground

Coming soon Solid Ground

Stand alones

For the Love of Chloe

Only Ever You

The Friends Duet

Loving Rowan

Three Days

The Forever Series

Something Real

The Right One

Unexpected

Chances Series

Another Chance

Taking Chances

Lifetime Series

In a Lifetime

In an Instant

In a Heartbeat

In the End

At the Start

ABOUT THE AUTHOR

Wendy Smith is a multi-platform bestselling author, whose book In the End, written as Ariadne Wayne, was named one of Apple's best books of 2017. She lives with her two children and two cats in New Zealand where she bases her books because she loves living there. All her stories come with a quirky sense of humour, and she cries over everything.

Find me online
www.wendysmith.co.nz
wendy@wendysmith.co.nz